Have Wand, Will Travel

Teresa J. Reasor

COPYRIGHT © 2018 by Teresa J. Reasor

Contact Information: teresareasor@msn.com

Cover Art by Tracy Stewart
Edited by Faith Freewoman

Teresa J. Reasor
PO Box 124
Corbin, KY 40702

First Edition Published by Amazon as part of the Magic And Mayhem Kindle World 10/17/2016

Publishing History: Second Edition 2018
ISBN 13: 978-1-940047-26-3
Print Edition

Table of Contents

Dedication

A special thanks to Author Robyn Peterman who inspired me to write this novella.

Originally part of her Kindleworld, this manuscript has gone through a large edit to insure every reference to her world has been removed. In order to do that, I have rewritten parts of the original manuscript and added to it.

And thanks to my editor Faith Freewoman and my cover artist Tracy Stewart. You both RULE!

Chapter 1

S TEALING FROM HUMANS was so easy. Too easy. Boring. That was probably why he'd stopped doing it ten years ago. Christophe leaned back against the rough brick of the Sutherlands' palatial home and became one with the shadows while he waited for the motion lights to go off.

Where was the excitement he'd experienced in the past when planning a job? Where was the thrill of slipping like a shadow, silent, unbreathing, through a house while its occupants slept?

With the advent of new technologies for security alarms and safes, he'd experienced a few moments when, had he had a beating heart, it would have given it a goose. But even that soon passed and became just another dull part of a humdrum job.

But a necessary one if he meant to keep his lights on. And that was another thing. It was so tedious to have to do this out of necessity, where before he'd done it as a sport or hobby.

Until he discovered where Arnold, his manservant, had

gotten to, however, he was strapped for cash. In the hundred years Arnold had been with him, he'd been unfailingly fastidious, honest, and responsible.

No, Arnold would never abscond with his money.

And there was another thing. Christophe could feel him close by, but couldn't pinpoint his location. He found it suspicious that as soon as he again managed to get close enough to reach the man, Arnold was suddenly somewhere else. And, based on the constant drain of energy from him to Arnold, Christophe suspected he was under considerable stress. Which he found worrisome.

As soon as he had the diamonds to fence, he'd find out what the hell was going on. He concentrated on the house.

At the recent unveiling of the new science building at the college, he'd run into Maxwell Sutherland by the hors d'oeuvres table and, with one concentrated glance, picked his brain for the code to open the safe and the location of the security cameras. People were getting more and more fancy toys to protect their property.

Bother.

He now opened his senses to every living thing within the house. He ignored the tiny mouse in the attached garage and her offspring and homed in on the humans. Five heartbeats palpitated inside his head. One's rhythm seemed out of sync, and he frowned. It wasn't the two adults he had followed for the better part of the evening during the unveiling ceremony at the college. Nor was it the nanny they paid to look after the children. He could sense her on the second floor. An adult's heartbeat was slower. There was an older child, six or seven. This one was hummingbird fast, but there was an irregularity. Did the parents know?

When the heartbeat stuttered he shifted uneasily. The rhythm leveled out and he relaxed again. Moving away from the side of the house, he eyed the windows overhead in an attempt to pinpoint which room was occupied by the stuttering heartbeat. He'd intended to go directly to the office, open the safe, lift the diamonds, and slip away. This new development threw a spanner in the works.

Hugging the shadows as he strolled around the side of the house, he used his excellent night vision to sidestep the large planters of flowers on the edge of the patio, and sidled up to the back door. Snapping on medical gloves, he withdrew his lock picks from the back pocket of his black dress pants. Inside the kitchen, the control panel next to the door lit up. He was at it, keying in the code, before it managed to beep. The panel went from red to green again.

He paused to listen to the heartbeats again. He always fed before a job so he wouldn't be distracted by hunger, but the sound still drew him. If he listened closely, he could hear the blood whooshing through their veins. All but that one small heart upstairs. It disturbed him.

An idea struck, and he wandered around the kitchen by the glow of a nightlight left on next to the sink. On the refrigerator he found a note pad for making lists and a pen tied to it with a string. Writing a quick message, he tore the piece of paper off and slipped it into his pocket.

Past the kitchen, a short hall opened into an open, tiled foyer with a broad, grand staircase leading up to a gallery above. It split into two sections, east and west. The tiny heart was in the east wing. He turned west.

Inside the Sutherlands' bedroom, he was greeted by the scent of expensive perfume and the sound of slow, even breathing on one side of the bed, and a whistling snore on the other. Surprisingly, it was Lorraine Sutherland making the noise. Maxwell, her husband was sleeping soundly and quietly.

The deep plush carpet cushioned the sound of Christophe's dress shoes as he glided to the dresser. He caught the glisten of metal and jewels in a decorative dish and smiled. His distended canines flashed in the mirror while he tucked the necklace into his pocket and propped the note he'd written about the baby's heart in its place. The possibility of getting caught had given him a small thrill. So few things did lately.

A movement came from the bed when Lorraine turned in her sleep onto her back. Her hand flopped against her husband's white belly. Mouth open, she gave a snort, followed by a rumbling snore that damn near got Christophe's heart started.

He streaked out the door and shut it behind him. How could such a diminutive woman make such a racket? He'd been on safari seventy years ago, and lions did not roar as loud.

Fifteen minutes later, Christophe exited the house with a velvet bag containing three pieces of jewelry. Aware of the numerous cameras in the neighborhood, he put on some speed as he ran across the smoothly manicured lawn to the patch of forest behind. All anyone would be able to see on the digital images was the motion-sensor lights flaring on.

Once concealed in the distant tree line, he slowed to a saunter and wandered east to where he'd parked his car.

He waved his hand as a mosquito the size of a canary buzzed his left ear.

Bloodsuckers.

He'd be drained if he didn't get a move on.

In the past, Arnold would have driven by to pick him up. His absence was both concerning and inconvenient. Where was he? And who was responsible for his disappearance?

He stepped out of the trees onto the deserted stretch of gravel road flanked on each side by partially completed houses. Surrounding his car were four darkly dressed beings. No heartbeats had warned him of their presence. The tallest stepped forward from out of the shadows into the glow of the streetlight. His pale, long face with its narrow black eyes, bony beak of a nose, and thin-lipped mouth triggered a rare feeling of dread.

Shit! The real bloodsuckers had arrived. And he knew instantly who had taken Arnold.

But why?

And what would it take to get him back?

Chapter 2

Z AIRA O'SHEA STUDIED the couple sitting in front of her desk. They were not her normal clients. For one, they were human, the biggest rarity. Two, they were wealthy and very well dressed.

Most of the shifters, due to...well, shifting, didn't wear *haute couture*, though most vampires came in decked to the nines. She'd often wondered if it was some kind of psychological thing about coffins and their Sunday best. But she'd never seen one carry a Louis Vuitton handbag like the one Mrs. Sutherland held on her lap.

The witches she'd handled cases for were middle income all the way. It was against the rules to use their power for financial gain. Unless you worked for it, like she was doing right now.

"What kind of burglar steals your jewelry and leaves a note about your baby?" Lorraine Sutherland demanded. "It was creepy enough that someone came into our home and stole from us, but to think he may have stood over our child and pressed his ear to her chest..." The small woman shuddered.

Zaira doubted he had done so. Shifters had acute hearing. Not as sharp as vampires. But it could have been either one.

"The house was quiet, and he probably tuned into the baby's breathing." Zaira O'Shea leaned forward in her seat, a pen poised over the legal pad on the desk. "What was it he wrote in the note?"

Maxwell Sutherland spoke for the first time. "Your baby's heart isn't functioning properly. You need to take it to a doctor immediately."

Not a shifter. A vampire, more than likely. From the formal wording in the note, possibly an older one. "And did you?" she asked. She'd never heard of a vampire with a soft spot for children. Could it be a female shifter?

"Well, yes," Lorraine said. "First I was afraid he'd done something to her, but I checked her over myself and there wasn't a mark on her. Then I got worried."

It was like pulling dragon's teeth getting information out of these people. "And?"

The woman's aura turned lemon yellow. She was worried, frightened for her child. Maxwell's turned a pale blue as he reached for his wife's hand and gave it a squeeze.

Lorraine continued, "Shelley was born with a hole in her heart. The doctor said it would close on its own, but she's developed a complication and had to have emergency surgery the next day. Had the burglar not left the note, we might not have noticed anything until it became critical."

"So in a sense, this burglar saved your child's life."

"Well, yeah. He stole at least three hundred thousand dollars' worth of jewelry, too," Maxwell said, his blond brows drawn together in a frown. Unlike most people making a living in construction, he had pale skin, lightly freckled.

His wife was as dark as he was light, with dark brown eyes and burnished, highlighted dark brown hair.

"Were you insured?" Zaira asked.

"Sure. And the insurance company has already made good on the claim."

"But you still want me to find out who he is?"

"Yeah." He nodded.

"Do you have pictures of the items that were stolen?"

"Yes, of course." Lorraine clicked open the clasp on her bag and dug around inside, finally pulling out an envelope and extending it across the desk. "There's a copy of the note in there, too."

Zaira opened the envelope, set aside the pictures and unfolded the more interesting note. The bold strokes of the penmanship had to be that of a man. He had printed the words, the lettering just shy of calligraphic. An older vampire. A vampire with sticky fingers and skills.

"If I can trace some of the pieces, I may be able to find him. I assume once I have, you want me to turn him over to the police."

"No!" The Sutherlands spoke together.

Surprised, Zaira leaned back in her seat.

"We don't want to cause him any trouble," Maxwell said. "The jewelry doesn't mean anything to us." His throat worked as he swallowed. "Three hundred thousand is a small price to pay for our daughter's life. She nearly went into cardiac arrest in the doctor's office. Had our burglar not warned us, she could have died in her sleep. We want to thank him."

Ten minutes later, with the contract signed for her services, Zaira saw the couple out. She stood at the large front window in the reception area and peered between the lettering. Maxwell Sutherland opened his wife's door and tucked her protectively into their BMW. It must have been a close call, indeed, if they were still clinging to each other.

A vampire with a soft spot for kids. She'd never heard of such a thing.

She shook her head and turned from the window to face the reception area of the office. She studied the wheat-colored walls and brown corduroy chairs, the dark walnut end tables and the clear glass lamps. The room looked professional and uncluttered.

And right now it felt empty. All the issues that plagued the human world were tripled with preternatural clients. Each species had their own special gifts. Drama and intrigue abounded, and sometimes violence. Risk was part of the job for her agents, and right now all six were out in the field dealing with cases.

Callista, their fairy, was embroiled in a particularly sticky case in which someone had imported a South American bird-eater tarantula to hold one family hostage inside their stump.

"Has everyone checked in today?" she asked.

Calamity, their receptionist, nodded. "Yes, everyone has called in."

"Is Callista okay?"

"Yes. She's fine. The spider has been captured. The EPA came in and got it. It seems it's illegal to import something like that for fear it will get a toehold here."

Zaira breathed a sigh of relief. "That's good to hear."

"Has she found out who imported the spider?"

"She's following the paper trail looking for proof to take before the Gnome Council. Seems it's a garden dispute."

When you had fairies and gnomes living in close proximity, there were always territorial issues. This one could have turned deadly.

With one last look around the reception area, Zaira noted with pleasure that Calamity had straightened the recent issues of Better Witch's Garden and Were Fashion Magazine (featuring tear-away clothing) on the waiting room tables and cleared her desk. Though at times the young witch lived up to her unfortunate name, she was slowly becoming competent.

This time when Calamity came in to announce a visitor, Zaira noticed her glow of excitement. The young witch almost vibrated with it.

"There are some people to see you. I've put them in the conference room because there are six of them."

"Six what?"

"Witches. Actually, one female and five males. The witch is gorgeous and powerful. I could feel her energy from across the room."

If she was projecting, she was doing it to show off or intimidate.

Not for Calamity's benefit, though, because she was very young and was just now coming into her power, so there'd be no reason to impress or intimidate her.

"Did they say why they're here?"

"They wish to hire you to recover something."

After so many years of dealing with all breeds of preternatural beings, it took more than a little residual power to shake Zaira. But six witches? Before she went into the room...well, it never hurt to hold her cards close to her chest.

She spent a few minutes in her office clearing her mind, setting up her defenses, and getting her legal pad. "Please let Cerbie out of his room, Calamity."

The woman shot her an anxious look.

"Everyone needs to pee," Zaira said.

Calamity did not look happy. "That's what I'm afraid of."

She bit her lip to keep from smiling. Her familiar had a

reputation for being difficult. "He actually likes you, so I'm sure he'll behave himself. If he doesn't, let me know, and he and I will have another of our come-to-Goddess meetings."

She pasted a smile on her face before stepping into the conference room to face the six. She took in the five dour faces of the males, who were dressed in the black robes of the Council, and her smile died. They looked like crows flocked around the table. This couldn't be good. Power lingered in the air like ozone after a lightning strike. She pushed her way through it as though she didn't notice, moved to an empty place at the table, and pulled out a chair, but didn't sit.

"I'm sorry you had to wait. I was in a meeting with other clients. What can I do for you?"

The only female witch in the room rose from her seat like Venus on the half-shell...or was it Marilyn Monroe? Because she was certainly dressed like Marilyn. Her makeup was applied with an artistry that would have taken hours if she were human. Platinum blond hair brushed her shoulders and curved beneath her chin as she turned her head, and she spoke in the girlish, breathy voice that had been part of Marilyn's persona. Zaira looked closely at her face. Damn. She really did look like Marilyn.

"We have come to you on a most urgent matter." Marilyn moved her shoulders in an unconscious affectation. It was she who was projecting the power. "But first I'd like your reassurance that you'll attend to this unfortunate event with the utmost confidentiality."

Zaira placed the pen she held on the pad. "Being circumspect is part of what we do here at the Have Wand, Will Travel Detective Agency, Miss—?"

Marilyn thrust out her bosom and drew a deep breath, making her breasts plump up that little bit extra. Every male eye in the room homed in on the result. Zaira almost heard them clicking in their sockets.

"Glendora Ghostly. I am right-hand assistant to the head of the Council of Magical Beings, Adira Nelson. She's on vacation, and has appointed me as temporary guardian of the Council until she returns."

The rapt expressions on the male witches' faces as they gazed at Glendora gave Zaira an uneasy feeling. All the birdlike Council members seemed mesmerized by the witch. There was something... While the cat was away, had the mice been playing naughty games? A high-pitched EW-WWW squealed inside her head, and she mentally shuddered.

She jerked her attention back to Marilyn/Glendora and decided, naw, it was all in the male heads sitting around the table. She heard Glendora say, "Something has gone missing during that time," and jerked her mind back to the issue at hand.

"A valuable artifact," Glendora breathed. "We didn't know it was gone until recently, so we have no way of knowing how long ago it was taken."

"I see. Was it kept in a locked storage area or a safe?"

"All important or rare documents and artifacts are kept in the Council's storage facility. All we have is the reference to it in our records, and the empty box in which it was kept."

"What kind of artifact is it?"

"A wand. A very old and valuable wand."

"Have you contacted your boss to ask her if she has loaned it out?"

The whole group stiffened and shot glances around the table like they were the targets and their thoughts the careening ball on a pinball machine. "No." One of the males who sat at the table spoke. "This is the first vacation she has taken since she became head of the Council. She was nearing exhaustion when she left, and we believe it would not be wise to interrupt it."

Zaira might have believed in his concern for Ms. Nelson's welfare if his attention hadn't kept wandering back to Glendora's cleavage.

"It is very unlikely that she would have loaned out such an important artifact," Glendora said. She raised one carefully arched brow. She pressed her hands together before her, increasing the swell of her breasts over the sweetheart neckline of her dress. Calamity was going to have to spend a bit of time cleaning the table to remove all the drool the five male witches were dripping onto it.

"The Council will see it as a great favor if you locate the wand and return it," Glendora concluded in her breathy tone, every word uttered in that sexy murmur.

Shit! She had been looking forward to finding the Sutherlands' vampire burglar. But it would not be wise to turn down the Council.

Adira Nelson was one of the most powerful witches in the country, and if something important had gone missing on her watch, she'd want it found...*now*. But why was her second-in-command projecting power? And why was her red aura clouded with black goo? The black goo associated with black magic.

This was so not good.

"I will need to examine the site where the wand was stored, as well as the container, and the records that refer to it."

Glendora smiled, well satisfied. "Of course."

"And you'll have to sign a contract hiring me, and pay my normal fee and any travel expenses."

Glendora snapped her fingers and one of the males was jerked to his feet as though he had a spring up his butt. "Archie, take care of the paperwork and the payment."

"Yes, mistress." He bowed.

Glendora snapped her fingers again and they were sailing along at mach speed to...

A library. Or at least that's what the large open room with its bookcase after bookcase of ancient-looking tomes and highly polished woodwork appeared to be. The smell of magic, like burned candles, incense, and ozone, lingered in the air. Zaira rocked on her feet for a moment upon landing, then found her balance.

Being hijacked to an unknown location was not one of her favorite experiences. Especially without warning. Defensive energy hummed through her, making her fingertips tingle and her face flash hot.

"I'm sorry for the quick exit, but you must understand, we have very little time to find the wand. Councilwoman Nelson could return at any moment. And I cannot allow you to know where this facility is. Only the Council woman and a few others are allowed to visit here."

Zaira cleared her throat and tried to swallow back her power, but her heart still raced. "I understand." She did not like this at all.

Glendora eyed her long tail of auburn hair. "You're a healing witch?"

"Yes." Among other things.

"Why would you become a detective?" she asked.

"Sometimes finding a missing loved one and healing a heart is just as important as healing a wound." Unless finding the loved one caused more pain, as it had in her case.

Glendora frowned, her eyes narrowed, as though she were working through a concept totally foreign to her. With a shrug she said, "Come this way."

They wandered through the cavernous but well-lit stacks, their steps echoing in the silence. Zaira was distracted by the large stained glass window overhead depicting goddesses from every culture arranged in a circle of protection.

Directly beneath it they came upon a large Louis XIV desk that looked very much like the real deal. A long wooden box with curved ends sat in the center of its polished surface. On the outside of the container, carved symbols twisted and turned as though alive.

Zaira approached the box slowly, because it was giving off a strange humming sound.

"It's been doing that ever since we found it," Glendora said.

"Have you opened it?"

"Yes. Nothing's in it."

Zaira placed a hand on the box and it immediately stopped humming.

"What did you do to it?" Glendora demanded, slightly panicked.

"Nothing. It's vibrating, and that's what's causing the sound."

"Why is it doing that?"

"I'm not certain. Perhaps from the movement of the symbols." She raised her hand and the box began to hum again. Perhaps it was calling to the wand. Zaira didn't want to suggest that to Glendora. There was something off about the woman. Why was she still projecting power, even though it was just the two of them?

"Is anyone on the Council out of touch other than

Councilwoman Nelson?"

Glendora's face blanked in shock. Then her expression took on a suspicious fierceness. "Yes. His name is Seymour Hurst. He left this afternoon on a scheduled trip for the Council."

"We don't need to jump to conclusions. I'll look him up first and rule him out as the thief, or capture him and bring him back. But if this was a scheduled thing, chances are he isn't our culprit. If it's someone who's discovered the location of this facility and they're not associated with the Council, you may need to strengthen your wards."

"Do you just capture and detain or do you go further?" Glendora asked.

Her blithe tone sent a chill down Zaira's spine. "I can do many things, but since I am a healing witch, killing is not one of them." Normally.

She'd heard about the torture the Council sometimes used. But surely they'd outgrown those Dark-Ages practices.

There was an edge to Glendora's voice that dispelled Zaira's comfortable belief when she said, "We will deal with the thief when you catch him."

"I'll need to take the box with me. And I need to see the provenance for the wand, and look around at all the entrances to the building."

"Certainly."

Zaira took a seat at the desk and studied the paperwork associated with the wand, noting that the paperwork was a copy instead of the original.

"The original document was so fragile we had to seal it away." Glendora explained. "What I've given you is a translation."

Created by a powerful witch in Ireland in the twelfth century, the wand siphoned power from those around it.

Most wands directed power with laser-like focus from the witch holding it. She'd never heard of one draining power from other beings and focusing it. No wonder it had been hidden here. It was more a weapon than a tool. And in the wrong hands it could be dangerous. The quicker she found the wand, the better.

"It would be helpful if I could call my familiar to me."

"Certainly," Glendora nodded.

Zaira brought Cerbie through with a thought. He arrived barking a stream of curses, his head thrown back as he snapped at the air, his teeth bared. He hated teleportation.

"That is your familiar?" Glendora looked at the twelve-inch-tall, tubby Jack Russell with something akin to horror.

"Yes. He's actually very talented." When he continued to growl his displeasure, Zaira narrowed her eyes. "Quiet, Cerbie."

The dog's growl lowered to a rumble in his chest, but his aggressive stance never changed. He eyed Glendora's shapely legs as though they were drumsticks and gave one a lick. The witch uttered a squeak, a look of disgust wrinkling her nose. She took a hasty step back.

"She tastes as good as she looks," Cerbie said.

Thank the Goddess she was the only one who could hear him. Fearful for his safety, Zaira said, "Nose to the floor, my little hell-hound. We have a thief to find."

His ears went up and his tongue lolled out the side of his mouth. He bared tiny, razor-sharp white teeth.

Zaira nodded. With Glendora snapping them from entrance to entrance, they were able to cover more ground, but they reached the last exit with nothing to show for their efforts.

"He didn't use a door to enter the facility," Zaira commented. "That leaves a window or one of the skylights. Which means our thief is either a witch, who teleported in, or someone or something else with skills." The word skills triggered a thought.

"How will you find him?"

"He's stolen an important artifact. He'll be looking for a market for it. I'll be looking for the buyer. I need to return to my office now, and I'll contact you as soon as I have news."

She didn't need Glendora's skills to teleport back to her office with Cerbie, the box, and the info.

As soon as she landed back in her office, she pushed the intercom. "Calamity, call Mr. and Mrs. Sutherland and tell them I'd like to look around their house and grounds."

Chapter 3

CHRISTOPHE STUDIED THE small, roughly-hewn wand. It had been fashioned from a single piece of oak, and was covered with carvings. It was also beautiful to look at, but to touch it bare-handed sent a crawling sensation through every part of his body. He had never held any weapon so dangerous. And he didn't intend to continue doing so.

He wrapped the wand in a towel, stifling its low-frequency hum, and secured it in a tube-like shipping container, further dulling the sound. He rose from his desk chair and rolled it back out of the way.

Kneeling before his desk, he lifted a section of the thick rug and pushed down on one of the floorboards. A small section of the floor popped up to reveal, half buried beneath it, a state-of-the-art safe. He keyed in the code. The lock released, and he lifted the door open, placed the container inside, and slammed it shut, breathing a sigh when he could no longer hear the hum.

With the safe closed, he returned everything to its place and sat back down to read the document once more. The words, though written in Gaelic, were plain enough. The wand was a weapon against the living dead. Vampires. It drained the power from them and directed it toward anyone the bearer chose, possibly other living dead, but not necessarily.

It was a common human misconception that vampires, because they were living dead, had no soul. But the power of this wand proved otherwise. It sucked the souls away from them, thus completing the process from living to completely dead. But it did one more thing. Instead of freeing the souls from the body and sending them on their way, it changed them into energy to be used against others.

One did not have to be a witch to use it. Theoretically vampires could use it against other vampires. There were those groups who had their own witch to call, who could instruct them in how to wield it against feuding vampire clans.

That alone was a monstrous concept.

But he had seen quite a bit of monstrous in his two hundred thirty years. More wars than he cared to relive. This one weapon could cause a civil war between witches and vampires, and throw the balance of power to the witches. Because every lost soul meant one less vampire. But he couldn't trust the Vampire Council any more than he could the Magic Council. They had proven again and again they weren't to be trusted. With great power came great abuses. And they were masters at it.

But how was he to get Arnold away from them? He

could track him, but the minute he got anywhere near the man, whoever held him teleported him somewhere else. It had to be a witch who was doing it. Vampires couldn't teleport. They could run fast enough to get from one place to another in a matter of seconds, but they hadn't the ability to scramble their molecules and shoot them through space.

Who could he get to help him rescue Arnold?

A vampire asking assistance from a witch would be immediately suspect. He needed a referral of sorts. He glanced at his watch.

Right now he had a meeting to attend. If all went well, he'd have the money to pay his light bill. He did like his creature comforts. And then he'd find a witch to help him rescue Arnold.

Using the rooftops and back alleys to travel ensured no one could follow, and he crossed the college campus to the other side of town in only a few minutes. He climbed from the roof down the fire escape to the back side of the jeweler's apartment building and tapped at his window. It was almost immediately opened from the inside, and he slipped through into the bedroom.

Milo Baig had been a fence for many years. And back in the day, Christophe had used him often. Since he'd given up the trade, he had no reason to until now.

Only four foot ten in his elevator heels, Milo seemed taller because of the confidence with which he carried himself. His kinky hair stood out from his head like steel wool, and his round face with his button nose and widely spaced blue eyes appeared always affable, and he listened with a kind smile and an expression of interest when anyone was speaking.

Knowing it was all a front, Christophe stayed alert while he was with the man. He'd been known to slip a knife between the ribs of someone he'd lost trust.

"There's a lot of interest in these jewels. They're calling you the babysitter bandit, did you know that?"

Christophe raised a brow. "I hadn't heard. I haven't read a newspaper lately." He'd been busy with his classes at the college. The semester was winding down and summer break only a week away.

"Did you really leave a note about the baby for the parents?"

"She was struggling. Her heart wasn't functioning correctly."

"How did you know?" The man seemed truly curious, an unusual event.

"Do you believe in the paranormal, Milo?"

"You mean spirits and stuff like that?"

"Only partly. There are certainly people who can sense the dead, and others who can move things with their minds."

"You really believe that shit."

"It's easier to believe in something when you have an ability of your own. I can sense illness in people. I know you may have to have a bypass in a couple of years. You really should get that checked out. You have a partial blockage on the left side."

Milo's mouth flew open, and he touched his chest. "You're just shitting me."

Christophe shook his head. "You're a good fence and an even better jeweler. I'd like to do business with you for many more years to come. Get it checked out, and you'll see if I'm right or not"

Milo paled a little. He turned to the business at hand. "I was able to ship some of the stones out a couple of days ago to one of my contacts. He got a good price for them. I took my regular ten percent." He extended an envelope thick with cash.

Christophe took the envelope and tucked it into the inside pocket of his black sports jacket. "I'll be awaiting news about the rest."

Milo's cell phone signaled a text had come through. He pulled it from his pocket as Christophe started out the window.

"Wait," Milo caught his arm and shook his head, his look eloquent with warning. "The police are on their way up."

A sinking feeling struck Christophe's stomach. The police hadn't been on the roof when he climbed in the window. He opened himself to everything in the building. Heartbeats raced as they came up the interior stairs. His own was threatening a beat or two as the need to escape rushed him.

"Are there cameras on your building?"

Milo shook his head. "No. Our security here sucks."

No cameras to worry about. But they'd be watching the fire escapes. He'd have to exit through another window. One they wouldn't be watching. He strode to the bedroom door and peeked out. No one was in the hall. A nicely decorated living room was visible from where he stood. He turned down the hall away from it and stepped into the bathroom with Milo close behind. He eased the narrow window open and unfastened the screen and handed it back to the man.

Poking his head out, he studied the sheer drop to the street, then looked up. The roof was just a few feet above the window. He'd done more difficult climbs.

As he started to duck his head out the window, Milo grabbed his arm. The man opened the medicine cabinet. It was empty. Then he grabbed an interior shelf and lifted out the entire back. Inside were stacks of bills bound with rubber bands.

Christophe raised a brow. Milo shrugged, "I may be out of business for a while. I'll get back to you when things cool down." He handed him one of the stacks. Christophe tucked it inside his jacket and offered his hand. The two shook. There was honor among thieves, but just in case, Christophe gazed into the man's eyes. "You will not remember me, my friend. I was never here. When I am gone, put the screen back in the window, secure the medicine cabinet, take a leak, and go back into the living room to watch television."

While Milo put everything back into place, Christophe wiggled through the window. He gripped the exterior frame with his fingertips and, using brute strength, lifted himself free of the narrow opening.

Climbing the exterior of an apartment building was much like rock climbing, something he had done many times in the past. Hooking his fingertips into the narrow cracks between the bricks, and wedging the toes of his running shoes between them, he was able to climb to the roof.

Stealthy and quiet, he hooked a leg over the molding at the top, swung himself over the edge, and froze. Nothing moved, and he heard no heartbeats. Rising, he backed away to get a run at the edge and leaped. He landed on the next roof nearly twenty feet away and ducked behind a ventilation stack just as the roof door across the way banged open. He lay back and looked up into the summer night sky, the moon just a sliver. He searched for constellations to calm the rush of adrenaline. There were Cassiopeia and Perseus. The Big Dipper and the Little one. He could barely see Orion because of cloud cover.

It was a real shame he'd been forced to dissolve a long-standing relationship in a matter of seconds because of a financial situation. Dammit. After several minutes, the sounds of searching finally ended on the roof and he eased up to see if the coast was clear.

"I think they're gone," a feminine voice said from behind him.

He jumped and twisted around. Red hair, large, cat-shaped eyes, a smile that was part smirk, part amusement. And she was a witch. He could smell the magic on her from where he sat.

"I didn't think vampires could be startled," she said, laughter in her voice.

"You used a cloaking spell. Otherwise you'd never have sneaked up on me. We're living dead. Any emotion you feel, we feel, but more."

"Why do you suppose that is?" she asked, her tone conversational and curious.

"Because we're caught between the moment of life and the moment of death all the time."

"I see you've given it some thought."

"Some." More than some. He'd had more than two hundred years to think about it.

He climbed to his feet and turned to face her.

She looked younger than he had at first thought, her skin smooth and glowing with health. She smelled wonderful. And the strong beat of her heart called to him. Though he'd fed before visiting Milo, the adrenaline had triggered a fierce need.

Her auburn hair hung in a long tail down her back. He imagined looping it around his hand and drawing her head back while he fed from her slender throat. He took a long step forward and came up against a barrier so strong he bumped his head and swore at the sudden pain.

"You're telegraphing your thoughts, vampire. I wasn't born yesterday."

Christophe rubbed the bruise on his forehead, but it was already healing. He lifted his arms to judge how close the barrier was. Shit, he was trapped. He rarely had to breathe anymore, but his chest expanded with quick hard breaths now, and his sluggish heart began to pound. "Are you with the police?"

"No. I just warned your fence they were coming. They must have discovered his connection to the jewels the same way I did."

His jaw tensed and he studied her again. "Why would you warn him?"

"Because my clients don't want you arrested. They want to meet with you and thank you for saving their child's life."

Ah. The baby.

"I just did you a favor. But if you'd like, I can call the police now." She shrugged and withdrew a cell phone. "The Sutherlands can meet with you at the jail as easily as my office."

"I would rather not," he said quietly.

At his tone she looked up to study him, then put the phone away. "Did you wipe Mr. Baig's memory?"

He quirked a brow. "What do you think?"

"Had you known him long?"

"A while." Why was she so interested? "For the most part, our relationship has been a legitimate one. I often bought antique jewelry from estate sales, and he would turn a profit from it."

"But not recently."

He didn't bother to answer. "Let me out of this cage."

"Not until we've come to an understanding."

"That I won't hunt you down and rip out your throat?"

That idea seemed to surprise her. "You'll leave a note for parents to save their child, but threaten a woman?"

"A witch holding me prisoner." He pushed his hands against the invisible barrier and turned to try and discover any weaknesses. The electricity of her magic tingled against his skin until it burned and he dropped his hands. His palms were blistered, but healed almost immediately. She couldn't kill him, but she could hurt him. "I will not meet the parents."

"Why not?"

"They'll recognize me."

Her brows rose. "You know them?"

"No." He could not explain. It would only pique her curiosity. He'd lose his job at the college. He'd once again be wandering, homeless. And what would happen to Arnold? "You said your clients, meaning the Sutherlands. You are not a policewoman or associated with the police?" He gained a small amount of satisfaction seeing wariness creep into her expression.

"If I don't meet with your clients, you won't be paid, will you?"

"No."

"If you can change my looks, perhaps I could meet with them." He knelt inside the cylindrical bubble, hoping to appear less a predator.

GODDESS, HE LOOKED like a fallen angel kneeling there with his dark curly locks tumbling about his ears, his well-trimmed beard, and those strange gray eyes glowing silver with first lust, then anger. His broad chest and shoulders looked powerful beneath his sports coat. His long legs were well muscled. They'd have to be, since he'd jumped the twenty-foot span between the buildings.

"What were you before?" she asked.

"Before what?" he asked.

"Before your transition?"

"A soldier, a husband, a father." His expression grew pensive and he looked away.

"Is that why you wrote the note? Because you had experience with your own children?"

He remained silent a moment. "Perhaps. Such a wee thing to struggle so."

"Did you go into her room?"

"No. Only the parents' room to leave the note."

"I'm sure the Sutherlands will be relieved to know that."

He shrugged. "Those who view us as monsters often behave with less humanity than we do. Are you going to leave me here to burn in the early morning sun over the theft of a few pieces of jewelry?"

She caught her breath, truly shocked at the notion. "No."

He looked up at her, his gray eyes still glowing. "That is a relief. There are those of your kind who would."

What he said was true. The witches and vampires had a natural dislike and wariness of each other. Witches drew their power from the life force around them. Vampires from the blood of the living. Which in a way was very similar. But she had seen inhuman actions on both sides. And keeping him imprisoned wasn't doing either of them any good. Besides, she needed him to be cooperative, not only to finish out the Sutherlands' wishes, but to answer questions about the break-in at the Council's storage facility.

"I'll be paid for finding you, whether or not you meet with the Sutherlands. But they really do wish to thank you. Their daughter might have died, had you not left that note. She had to have emergency surgery the next day."

"I'm glad they followed through on my suggestion."

"And you did steal three hundred thousand dollars' worth of jewelry from them."

Three hundred thousand! He rose to his feet. "You're kidding me right?"

His change from his normal formal way of saying things to a more colloquial vocabulary caught her attention. "What do you mean?"

"The Sutherlands are pulling a fast one on you, or the insurance company, or both."

He spoke with such conviction she was tempted to believe him. "If the police have traced the gems you gave to Mr. Baig, there will be a record."

"And if the Sutherlands are in financial difficulty, there will be a record of that as well."

"So how much would you say what you took was worth?"

"Hypothetically, if I had done the job…"

She fought the urge to roll her eyes.

"Three necklaces and a bracelet worth twenty-five thousand max. The rest of what Mrs. Sutherland wears is fake."

That was two hundred and seventy-five thousand dollars' profit Sutherland would collect from the insurance company, if what this thief said was true.

But what had Sutherland done with the original gems?

Possibly the same thing this vampire had done. Brought them to Mr. Baig or someone similar to sell, replaced the diamonds with fakes, and the insurance company would be none the wiser, as long as he had the receipts for the original pieces and photos of them to authenticate his ownership. And they had handed her photos of the pieces during their first meeting.

Shit! And she had liked the Sutherlands. Damn them!

She dropped the shielding she'd used to cage the vampire, but kept her eye on him.

He reached out to feel for the barrier and, finding it gone, stuck his hands into his pockets and relaxed. Damn him, he looked like a GQ ad. Model-gorgeous and masculine as hell. He even had a little charm. Too bad he didn't have a pulse.

She pointed a warning finger at him. "Don't try using any of your vampire woo-woo on me. It won't work. I'm immune to it."

He bowed his head and flashed her a fanged smile that shouldn't have been charming, but was. "I will keep my woo-woo to myself."

The way he said it made it seem about something more than his ability to compel. Her cheeks burned.

"How much are they paying you to find me?" he asked.

"Five thousand dollars."

"They may have more in mind than a thank-you, since I know about the jewelry."

"Let me recover from one disappointment before you pile on another, will you?" It was depressing to discover your clients weren't exactly what you expected them to be.

He smiled, and with his fangs retracted and in the soft glow of the security lights, he looked human. But he wasn't, she warned herself.

And there was no proof what he said was true. But she

would look into the Sutherlands' finances, just in case. Dammit.

"So you're a private detective?" he asked.

"Yes."

"And a witch."

"Yes."

"You're exactly what I need at the moment."

Wow, the gall of some people. "If that's a pickup line, you can forget it."

"No. It wasn't."

Now she felt a little insulted.

"Not that you're not attractive enough for me to want to pick you up, but I need a witch who'll help me rescue someone very important to me."

Chapter 4

"IF YOU'RE NOT going to turn me into the police, perhaps we could go to a coffee shop and have something to drink," Christophe suggested. Now it was dark, the temperature had dropped, and she looked chilled. The smell of car exhaust from down on the street lingered in the air. "It will give me an opportunity to explain why I stole the jewelry from the Sutherlands, and why I need a witch. And it will give you time to see I'm not the monster you think I am."

She studied him with a dubious frown. "You were going to bite me, and now you want me to have coffee with you?"

"It was a momentary lapse. I promise not to bite you while you drink your coffee. It would be rude."

She laughed, then sobered as he strolled forward. The defensive tension built in her body language. In his most soothing voice, he said, "I work with humans all the time and am able to control my," he grinned, "woo-woo. You needn't be afraid. We can help each other, perhaps."

"You steal for a living, and you want me to trust you?"

"I work for a living. I've just run up against something

untoward and resorted to a little burglary to resolve the issue."

Her brows rose at that.

He motioned toward the door leading down into the apartment building.

"I'd prefer you go first."

Trust was going to take some time with this one. It was a shame he couldn't use his vampire woo-woo on her. He wanted to laugh every time he thought it. Instead, he shrugged and headed for the door.

The Dish wasn't exactly bustling at almost midnight. Four students were pulling a late-night study session in one of the booths, and a couple had fallen asleep from exhaustion at their tables. The wait staff, used to the last-minute insanity of the semester, worked around them, cleaning up, refilling salt and pepper shakers, and rolling silverware for the next day.

"We don't have much time. The diner will be closing in half an hour, so I'll get right to it. A month ago, Arnold, my uncle, disappeared. Someone took him while I was at work. Arnold has been with me for...a very long time. I have trusted him with all my financial issues because he's more...human, and people are more at ease with him. Everything is direct deposit these days. No one ever hands you a paycheck anymore and says 'go, you earned it, spend it.' But when he disappeared, it left me without access to any funds. I didn't know how much money it would take for me to hire people to help me get him back, so I chose someone I thought could afford a small loss."

Over her shoulder, he saw Andy Kutzerd, one of his students, swagger into the diner and go to the counter to place an order. He was hard to miss, with his carrot-red hair and six-foot-three frame. He played football on the college team, their star quarterback. Happily, his usual entourage of fellow players and girls were not in attendance.

He knew the kid, since he was in Christophe's American History class, and unfortunately the booth wasn't big enough for Christophe to duck out of sight. Andy would be bearing down on them at any moment. Shit. This night was getting more and more interesting. "Excuse me for a moment." He slid free of the booth and approached the student. "Hello, Andy."

"Hey, Professor. How you doin'?"

"I'm fine."

"Beautiful lady you're with," Andy said, his curiosity palpable. "Girlfriend?"

"Hopefully. First date." It was impossible not to grin at that.

Andy grinned in return. "You know most of your students think you're gay. There's rampant interest. Bets and everything going on. You just gave me an edge."

Christophe shook his head. "Why would my personal life be of interest to the student body?"

"Well, all the girls flock around you after class, but you

never show any interest, even when they go into overdrive and try to vamp you. And you do live with that older dude."

Christophe coughed to cover his single bark of laughter at the vamp comment. "That older dude is my uncle." Or at least that was the cover he and Arnold both used when questions were raised about their living arrangement. "And I don't show interest in the ladies in class because it's against university policy to date students. And they're much too young for me."

"Policy is policy, but if I had that kind of interest..." Andy peeked around Christophe's shoulder again, then shrugged one massive, muscular shoulder.

"You'd be out of a job. And I'm rather attached to mine. It pays the bills."

Andy grinned. "Point taken, Professor. But you have a stronger will than I have."

Or maybe he was just getting old. Hell, he was old. He bit back a sigh.

"Is there something I can do for you?" Andy asked.

"Yes, there is." Christophe debated with himself about how much to affect the student's memory. He decided to give him a gentle nudge, gazed into the man's eyes, and projected his will. "Stay here at the counter and give us some privacy."

"Sure thing, Professor," Andy nodded.

Christophe wandered back to the table.

"Afraid I'll figure out where you work?" she asked as

soon as he sat down.

"You'll figure it out soon enough. My name is Christophe, but you may call me Chris if you like." He offered his hand.

She hesitated then accepted it, shook it briefly and said, "Zaira." She twisted her coffee cup around in a circle. "Why don't you continue with what you were saying?"

"I've been tracking Arnold for a month, but every time I get close, they move him before I can reach him. It has to be witches."

"Why would they take him?"

Christophe shoved a hand through his hair, pushing back his curly locks. If he told her too much, she wouldn't help him. If he told her too little, it would put her in danger. "To force me to do something I don't want to do. They're holding Arnold hostage until I do it."

"What is it they've asked you to do?"

"I can't tell you what it is."

"Have you done it yet?"

"No. But if I can free Arnold and get him somewhere safe, I can tell them to go stake themselves."

"If you can't get him to safety, what then?"

"I'll have to do what they've demanded. Or they'll kill him."

"Why do you think witches are holding him?"

"Vampires can run very fast, making it appear as though we get from point A to point B in a matter of seconds.

Arnold is very old, but he's still human. He wouldn't be able to run. And his position change is instantaneous."

"Like a witch teleporting?"

"Yes."

She was silent for a long moment.

He stared at the small crease between her auburn brows in fascination. Her eyes were hazel, a blend of green and brown, with touches of blue around the iris. Her skin was almost as pale as his, but flawless, and it had the warmth of the living to give it more glow. A tender blush rose to her cheeks, telling him she'd noticed his masculine interest.

"I'll come in and meet with the Sutherlands under a disguise spell, if you'll help me get Arnold back, and I'll pay you whatever fee you decide is fair. I can narrow it down to his general area, but you'll have to locate him. Then you can teleport me to the location before they can escape with him."

"It would be easier if I could go in alone. If you come with me, they may sense you before we arrive."

"It's too dangerous for you to go in alone. You won't be dealing with witches alone. There are vampires involved. With both working together…it would be too risky."

"I've never known vampires and witches to work together. What could be so important they'd agree to do that?"

Christophe swore, his gaze latching onto the two vampires entering the diner. "We need to go." He grasped her wrist and slid out of the booth fast, pausing to toss a bill on their table. She tensed in resistance until she looked over her shoulder and saw the two large vampires bearing down on them.

"Hold onto me," she demanded, grasping his jacket.

Christophe slipped his arms around her waist and held her tight against him. He experienced the sensation of flying, but he was blind to where they were going.

He staggered back against a wall as they came to a halt inside an office, his hands sliding down over her firm, delectable bottom.

Zaira, unbalanced, leaned against him, her head tucked beneath his chin. His heart was actually beating from the magic she'd expelled...or was it her breasts pressing against his ribs, or the elemental scent she emitted, a blend of cinnamon, woman, and ozone?

It had been a long time. And he was dead, not blind or numb.

She looked up at him and those tricolored hazel eyes settled on his face. "That had better be a banana in your pocket."

Christophe chuckled, straightened, and released his tight grip with some reluctance. "I found my first teleportation—stimulating."

"Yeah, right." Zaira took a decisive step away from him, her eyes avoiding his and her cheeks flushed.

A hoarse, grumbling growl sounded from down the hall. A high-pitched bark preceded the sudden appearance of a white sausage with a nose on one end and a stub of a tail at the other. A ridge of hair stood up along the dog's spine as he advanced on Christophe, stiff-legged and decisive, his growls growing in volume the closer he got.

"I don't think I've ever seen anything built so close to the ground with such a ferocious attitude," he commented. "I take that back. Perhaps a badger I ran into one time while hunting."

"I wouldn't insult my familiar if I were you. He understands every word you say."

"That wasn't an insult. Badgers are quite aggressive creatures."

Said aggressive badger sniffed his shoes and pant leg, then proceeded to lift his leg. With lightning-quick vampire reflexes, Christophe jumped back, barely managing to avoid the stream of urine. "Hey!"

"Cerbie, that trick is getting very tiresome," Zaira said with a sigh. She waved her hand to clean up the spot on the carpet.

Christophe narrowed his eyes. Was that a wisp of smoke coming off the carpet? What was that pooch peeing?

The Jack Russell pranced off with a satisfied growl to stand next to Zaira in a protective, vigilant manner. He grinned, showing tiny, sharp, white teeth.

Christophe flashed his fangs, then realized he was having a face-off with a twelve-inch tall dog and quickly closed his mouth. Luckily, Zaira seemed distracted by her familiar.

Her attention shifted back to him. "Who were those two goons?"

"They were the assistants to the head of the Vampire Council, Ignatius Adcock."

"Adcock? So a vampire is holding your uncle prisoner? Not witches."

"I think vampires are holding him with the help of witches."

"Don't you think you should tell me what it is they've asked you to do?"

"No. It's in your best interest not to know." It would only confuse the issue. She'd want the wand back to sway power in the witches' direction. He wanted to protect vampire kind. The Council wouldn't care. Their agenda was to strengthen their positions no matter the cost to the rest of the vampires they were sworn to protect. He'd seen it happen in the past.

Regardless how they threatened him or Arnold, he'd never be able to give the Vampire Council the wand. It had to be hidden away or destroyed.

Destroyed would be the best thing. So why wasn't he heading home right now to end this whole thing?

Because he cared about Arnold, and if he was punished or killed...Arnold was the only person in his life. The only person he trusted, and who trusted him implicitly. He'd known him a hundred years. To lose him would leave a huge, terrible void in his life.

He looked up to see Zaira studying him and realized he'd been standing for some moments in thought.

His concern must have been plain, for she asked, "How do you know they haven't already killed him?"

"I can feel him out there to the west. But I can't pinpoint where."

"They may be attempting to cloak him. But their spell isn't strong enough, because your bond is too strong. If I'm to locate him, I'll need some of your blood."

He knew she'd be able to do a number of things with his blood. Including locate him, wherever he might be. His work and home life would be an open book to her. He needed to avoid that if possible. "Wouldn't some of Arnold's blood be more helpful?"

"Yes, actually, it would."

"I can fetch it now or bring it to you tomorrow."

"I won't be able to do the locator spell until tomorrow, so that will be soon enough."

Another thought occurred to him. "Adcock's goons saw your face. They will be looking for you to discover what part you play in my life. You need to be very careful."

"I will. I can ward my office to keep any vampire from entering unless invited. My home is already protected."

"Very well. I will return tomorrow." But now that they were parting, he was reluctant to leave.

Zaira took the decision out of his hands by stepping to the desk and retrieving a business card. She wrote a number on the back. "Call before you come, since I'll need to invite you in."

If only she would. He was still stiff as a poker and craving a release he hadn't had, or desired, in a very, very long time. "Take care, Zaira." He nodded to her, gave her dog a wide berth, and strode out the door.

With every step he was wishing he'd tasted her lips before releasing her. She'd have probably fried him for doing so. It might have been worth it.

ZAIRA WATCHED FROM the window while Chris strode down the street, his long-legged strides purposeful and graceful. Why was it vampires seemed to have a natural grace to their movements few humans did? Did death cause that?

As a witch, she had responsibilities to family, friends, Cerbie, and her business. Those were weights she accepted and carried without giving them a second thought. They were a part of her. But with his transition from human to vampire, Chris had probably shed all of that, or outlived it. His family was probably dead. All but Arnold. She'd read the concern in his expression. The man was obviously very important to him, beyond his responsibility for the vampire's financial issues.

Chris seemed very alone. Although he had approached that young man at the diner. But their body language indicated he was in a position of power over the human, possibly a mentor or something. Not a boss. The younger man's aura had reflected that.

Cerbie's growl brought Zaira's attention back from the window. "What did you think?"

He sniffed and tossed his head, his attitude dismissive.

"I think he may be the one who stole the wand, Cerbie. He certainly has the skills."

Cerbie growled conversationally, "Yeah, I noticed that when he had his hands on your ass and you weren't even protesting."

"He was holding onto me because we were teleporting."

He raised both his ears. "Is that what you call it now?"

Guilt stung her cheeks. She hadn't minded Chris's hand on her ass, and the response of his body to hers had been...bigger than a banana, and triggered a very interesting response. It opened up a whole jumble of questions about vampire stamina and whether he bit during sex.

She was not falling into bed with a vampire. No way, nohow.

They were the bad boys of the supernatural world. Like James Dean, but without a motorcycle, because they didn't need one.

She'd outgrown the thing she'd had for dangerous bad boys in the past. She wasn't going to pick it back up.

Too bad male witches left so much to be desired. They were total duds in the sack. She'd had enough wham-bam-thank-you-ma'am experiences, all two of them, to last a century. Their idea of foreplay was to encourage a witch to grab their wand and then say "make a wish."

She spoke aloud, hoping to convince herself and Cerbie. "Even if I was interested, vampires and witches are not a good blend. There are tensions between our species and our Councils. Remember the flack I caught for hiring Roger to handle the vampire cases?"

He grunted. "You could turn this over to Roger."

"I can't. The Council of Magical Beings came directly to me to recover the stolen wand. They don't want anyone else involved. They'd have a conniption if I brought a vampire into their circle. That's why we have Aileen to deal with Pixie cases, Calista to deal with Fairies, Roger to deal with Vampires, and Patrick to deal with the Shifters." She switched direction. "Did Chris smell familiar to you?"

"No. But when we were at the Council storage facility all I could smell was Marilyn's perfume and her magic."

"Glendora's," she corrected him automatically.

"Whatever."

"If he isn't the one who stole the wand, maybe he can help me figure out who did. I mean he's in the business, though he implied it was a one-time thing."

"Sure, and if you believe that, I have a patch of slightly withered but well-fertilized grass out back I'll sell you real cheap."

Zaira straightened. "Yes, about that. Really, Cerbie. Even Calamity is skittish about you peeing on her. If you can't control your impulses, I may have to install a dog house and fence in your patch of grass out back."

"You wouldn't!" he barked.

She narrowed her eyes. "I'm growing tired of cleaning up your adolescent messes. We both know you're no longer a child, and haven't been for some time. It was amusing the first one or two hundred times, because of who you chose to do it to, but now it's become a nuisance."

He raised one brow and gave her his pitiful Cerbie look.

"After a hundred years together, that expression has run its course, too."

He sniffed and turned his head. "You can be a real witch sometimes, Zaira."

"You can be a real hellhound, too."

He gave her his most evil grin, showing all his teeth. "But you love me."

Yeah, she loved those bad boys. That brought her right back to Chris, his fallen angel looks, and his banana. Or was it a zucchini? She hadn't had time to make a judgment.

No bad boy vampire for her. No way, nohow.

Chapter 5

CHRISTOPHE STUDIED THE catastrophic damage to his home in horror. Every drawer's contents had been dumped and destroyed. Every mirror broken. Every article of clothing he owned ripped to shreds. His couch was slashed, and the stuffing pulled out, and the mattresses on every bed had received the same treatment. The windows had been stripped bare of curtains and shades. There was not one piece of furniture that remained unblemished. And every book in his library had been ripped to pieces.

To be done in the length of time he'd been gone, it had required more than one person to do it.

But they had not found the wand. He'd checked first thing while the cops were upstairs.

The neighbors had called the police, and he stood back while they documented the damage. Even the hardened street cops were amazed at the destruction.

"Did you piss some students off, Professor?" the taller of the two police officers asked. "It doesn't look like they were here to steal anything. It looks as though someone was really pissed off and had a party here."

"We don't have our semester exam until tomorrow. No one's failed the class yet, and I haven't had words with any of them. I really don't know who could have done this."

"Would you mind if we call our forensic guys in to take a look? If this isn't a random thing it, could get messy, and it would be best for us to get the guys before they do this to someone else's home."

"No. Bring them in. It's not as if I can go to bed."

Christophe settled in his slashed desk chair over the section of flooring that covered the safe and propped his feet on the open hole at the bottom where the lowest desk drawer should have been.

He took stock of everything he'd lost, and decided the only things he regretted were a few first edition books given to him by a very old friend who'd passed away long ago, and a hundred-year-old photograph of his second wife, Lynette, a human. It was all he had left of their relationship besides his memories. Why hadn't he put it in the safe?

Because he'd never dreamed the Vampire Council would go to such spiteful lengths. Did they know he'd already stolen the wand and hidden it? Were they systematically destroying everything he had to force him to turn it over?

Or had the two goons sent after him taken it upon themselves to destroy the place before returning to the Council empty-handed?

Or were they preparing to do something worse?

Everything was gone. He tried to close off his feelings to that.

But it mattered, very much. This had been their home, his and Arnold's. They had taken his friend and destroyed his home.

He remained in the chair when the police arrived to take fingerprints and photograph the place, his rage building.

One of the technicians took his fingerprints, then loaded his stuff up to leave. "There's a company you can hire to clean up the mess, Mr. Bakas." He handed him a card.

"Thank you."

"We got some good prints. If they're in the system, we'll get them."

"I hope you do." There wasn't a chance in hell.

"You're calmer than I would be if I'd come home to this."

He looked up at the man. "I'm not calm at all."

The man turned white and backed away. "If you think of anyone who might have done this, you need to call the police and tell them. Don't try to take things into your own hands."

He nodded and turned his thoughts inward once again. At least the rubble had prevented them from finding the safe and the wand. It would be a cold day in hell before they'd get it from him. He'd beat the thing into splinters and burn it first.

He waited for the men to leave and rose, stiff after sitting for so long. Every step he took, he crunched across something that had belonged to them.

He needed to feed. He couldn't be around humans if he didn't. And he needed to gain control of his temper. He could not return to Zaira's office if he wasn't under control. He wondered if the goons—Zaira chose that word well— had discovered the hidden refrigerator in the kitchen. There had been so many other things destroyed, he hadn't bothered to look. But now he needed blood.

He shuffled through the destruction and went into the kitchen. Broken bottles of wine from the wine fridge littered the floor. He had collected some very fine wines in the past few years, his one indulgence, since he lived on a liquid diet. He took a breath and smelled the bouquet of several mixed with pickles and mustard. A deep sigh of regret escaped him. He opened the pantry. Cans of soup, a favorite of Arnold's, lay crushed, their contents mixed with pasta and rice, flour and sugar.

Shoved back beneath the wide bottom shelf was the refrigerator. He opened it and found the bags of blood undisturbed. The microwave had been destroyed, its door ripped off, so he drank it cold, standing at the counter.

Daylight came more quickly than he needed. He took a bag of Arnold's blood from the refrigerator. On occasion he drank some to renew the bond between them, but for the most part it was stored in the event Arnold was injured.

He cleaned up as best he could at the kitchen sink and

brushed his teeth with his finger coated with salt and baking soda, the only toothpaste he could find. After washing his hands, he called his teaching assistant at the college and asked him to administer the final test, then called Zaira. "I'm on my way to deliver the blood."

"I'm arriving at the office now. I'll be watching for you."

"Thank you."

He hung up abruptly. He hadn't even gone to look in the garage to see if they had damaged his car. His rage was already reaching stratospheric proportions before he ever reached for the door. *If they'd put so much as a fucking scratch on his car, he was going to rip their throats out.*

Luckily it hadn't occurred to the vandals to include the garage in their demolition. They probably didn't drive. Few vampires did. He slid into his classic Aston Martin DB5, started the engine, hit the electronic opener to raise the garage door, and shot down the drive.

Aware of the danger he might bring to Zaira's door, he cruised around town to make sure he wasn't being followed, then whipped into her parking lot and parked alongside a large van in the side lot, using it for cover.

He had barely gotten out of the car when she poofed beside him. "Oh, my Goddess, an Aston Martin?"

For the first time since he'd left Zaira last night he had something to grin about. "Yes, it is." The excited adoration in her expression and unwavering focus on the vehicle was nothing short of manic.

✧　✧　✧

"I HAD ONE years ago. Just like this. Don't you just love that dull, silver-toned paint?" Zaira ran a hand over the molded shape where the headlight fit into the front of the vehicle, then rubbed her sleeve over where she'd touched it to remove the fingerprints.

"Would you like to go for a ride?" Christophe asked.

After she'd sworn to herself she was going to keep her distance, he had to pull up in this particular car. "Could we?"

"Sure. It might be better if we conduct business outside of town anyway."

She was already sliding into the passenger seat as he spoke and he chuckled. He got into the vehicle. "I installed the seatbelts myself. I didn't trust anyone else to do it right."

"Wise decision. You can't turn these things over to just anyone." She ran a hand over the dash then wiggled back into the seat.

She turned to find Chris biting his bottom lip, his strange gray eyes glowing silver.

"Are you okay?"

"Yes. I'll tell you about it once we get out of town."

He backed out of the parking spot and pulled into traffic, traveling with the flow of cars down Main Street, then turning onto West Karma. They passed large two-story houses, some as old as the town, and meandered onto the entrance ramp to a bypass that circled Scryville. They remained silent as Chris hit the gas and they sailed down the four-lane road, the car hugging the curves. She loved the feel of the powerful engine speeding them through the mountain pass. Chris's hands rested lightly on the wheel, his attention focused on the road.

Her attention had finally drifted from the car back to him. His long fingers gripped the steering wheel with careful control. Vampires were known for their brutality, not sensitivity. But Chris had piano player's hands, poet's hands. What would his touch be like while making love?

She jerked her thoughts back from their libido-clouded haze with a *bad witch, bad witch. Bad, sexually-deprived witch.*

"How is it you became a private investigator?" he asked, interrupting her fixation.

She cleared her throat. "When I was a very young witch, I became obsessed with finding my father. Male witches are a bit like bull elephants." He shot her a look, and she shook her head and rolled her eyes.

"Not like that. I just meant that they have a tendency to spread their seed and then move on. So when he disappeared, my mother wasn't concerned. They weren't married, and their affair had burned out. But I missed him. He was funny and loving, and I just couldn't believe he'd leave me without some kind of farewell. As soon as I came into my power I started looking for him."

"And you found him?"

"What was left of him." She tamped down the emotion

that threatened to overwhelm her. "He had a house in the mountains here. He'd been murdered and left in a cave near his home. His killer, whether human or preternatural, has never been caught. But one day I'll find out who did it and see to it my father gets justice."

"I'm sorry, Zaira." His voice deepened in sympathy.

"Thanks." She turned the conversation back to him. "You're out in the sun. How is that possible?"

"I'm two hundred and thirty years old. The older we get, the more resistance to the sun we have. I still have to wear sunscreen, and I can't stay out in it for long periods. Inside the car, I'm fine. Plus I had a special tint applied to the windows to shield me."

"You're still dressed in the same clothes from last night. Haven't you been to bed?"

He shook his head. "They destroyed my house."

She caught her breath. His calm tone sent goosebumps up her arms. "They?"

"I think it was the two goons from last night. When they couldn't get me, they decided some payback was in order to make it very clear how serious they were."

"What do you mean destroyed?"

"Every piece of electronics, every picture, every book, every stick of furniture was systematically ripped or hacked or stomped to pieces. There's nothing left that hasn't been demolished. They even dumped out the refrigerator and ripped the doors off every appliance."

Her stomach hollowed out at the thought. She pressed a hand to her mouth, though words completely escaped her. She finally managed, "I'm so sorry. If you'll take me by your house, I may be able to reconstruct some of it."

He glanced at her. "Don't you have to have a working knowledge of what you reconstruct?"

"Some things. I don't have to have a working knowledge of how a book is constructed to know how it goes together."

He reached inside his jacket and took out a bag of blood. He placed it in her lap. "It's more important that we find Arnold. Once he's safe, I can deal with the rest."

The blood was still cool from the refrigerator. She rested a hand on his arm, but was immediately flooded with his anger and pain, so she withdrew her touch.

The empathic part of her that worked hand-in-hand with her healing caused her a great deal of trouble. By keying into a person's emotions, she learned about them more quickly than through conversation. She didn't want that with Chris.

If it was as she suspected, and they were both after the same thing, it would put them at odds with each other. She'd find it hard not to take his needs into consideration when it came time to turn the wand over to the Magic Council. But she knew one thing. She couldn't stand by and allow a man to be killed, either.

She touched the bag of blood. "We need to pull over so I can work a locator spell."

"Here, in the middle of nowhere?"

She looked around at the mountain scenery on either side of them. "What better place to draw from the power of nature? All I need is a map and this blood."

"There's a map of the area in the glove box."

Turning the small knob on the compartment door, she opened it, removed the map, and studied it. It was a map the chamber of commerce gave out to tourists. Perfect for what they needed.

Chris turned onto a gravel road leading up into the mountains. The small car, built very low to the ground, wasn't built for mountainous terrain, and they bounced for several minutes along the trail that was more of a path. Finally, he pulled over onto a widened, flat patch of dirt kept free of grass and trees by vehicles allowing drivers going the other direction to pass.

The two of them released their seat belts, got out, and met at the front of the car. Zaira spread the map out on the hood of the vehicle. "I need something I can use to pierce the bag."

Chris took the bag from her, extended his fangs and bit it, then handed it back to her.

Her attention snagged on him. Dear goddess, even with his fangs out he was hot.

She was not falling for a vampire. No matter how hot he was.

She had to keep reminding herself he was a thief, so it would be an entirely inappropriate, as well as colossally stupid, move.

She squeezed out a small amount of the blood onto the map and handed him the rest.

She ran her hands back and forth just above the map while she drew her power from the things around her. She tasted the greenery of the trees, bushes, and plants upon her tongue, and another, spicier flavor that could only be him.

"Blood of friend, we will send,

"To the place he rests, or nests.

"We will find

"Where he is forced to hide.

"Where might he be? So mote it be."

The blood beaded into a ball and started rolling toward the east side of town, coming to a stop in the center of Hallows Drive.

"Give me sight, before my flight," she murmured and opened herself to a vision of the place. A man was bound in a chair by heavy ropes, his white hair disheveled and lank, as though he hadn't combed or washed it in days. His skin had an unhealthy pastiness to it. She felt the pain in his wrists and ankles where the bonds cut into his frail skin. Felt the hunger that gnawed at his belly. His weakness. Why were they not caring for him? He wouldn't last much longer in such conditions.

Chris's hand clamped over her shoulder.

"I can't bring you both back with me at once. If I take

you with me and have to leave you, we'll just be exchanging one bad situation for another."

She sensed the tug of war inside him. "Get him," Chris urged, and released her.

Zaira took flight, speeding to the man. Her sudden appearance startled him.

His eyes shifted and widened. "Watch…" he started to speak.

"Fracus!" Zaira shouted, throwing out a burst of power and creating a bubble around them. She felt an answering power hit the shield and ricochet away. She turned to face her attacker, only to find an empty room. The witch was gone. But she couldn't drop her shield yet. She might be hidden and waiting for Zaira to do just that.

She threw out a hand, and the ropes holding Arnold to the chair fell away. He groaned. She turned to examine him.

"I'm all right, Miss. It's just the blood rushing back in after so long. Hurts some." His aristocratic English accent sounded so posh. "I assume Master Christophe sent you."

"Yes. I'm going to get you out of here as soon as possible."

"If there are any more witches about, Master Christophe can hear their heartbeat."

"Not if they're hiding under a cloaking spell." She thought of Cerbie, and he appeared just outside their bubble, gnashing his teeth. "Look around, Cerbie, and see if anyone else is here."

He growled as he scented the air and circled the room. He sneezed and shook his head. "The coast is clear."

"Are you able to stand, Arnold?" Concerned at how shaky he was while he struggled to his feet, she looped his arm across her shoulders, then thought of Chris and the car, and they were zooming to him.

Arnold's legs collapsed and he started to fall as soon as they landed. Chris leaped forward and caught him and held him steady. "You're safe now, Arnold."

"I knew you'd find me and get me out."

At Cerbie's bark of warning, Zaira threw up another shield, but it was just a pickup coming down the trail.

The truck squeaked to a stop. The man pushed his battered baseball cap back with hand. "You folks lost?"

"No. We just stopped to let the dog out for a moment," Zaira explained. Cerbie hiked his leg on the guy's tire to demonstrate, then trotted over to stand next to her.

The driver waved and rolled on down the hill.

"His tire's not going to go flat from the battery acid your dog urinates, is it?" Chris asked.

"No. Is it, Cerbie?"

The Jack Russell snorted in reply and turned to present his white butt and stubby tail to them both. It looked very much like he'd just flipped them off.

Chapter 6

"I'M VERY SORRY, sir. I went out to the market. I was putting the groceries in my car when these two huge vampires grabbed me and threw me into a van. And they put a sack over my head so I couldn't see where we went. It was a house, in the hills, I think, because the road sloped upward. But I was only there for a few days.

"There was a woman there who brought me food now and then. Just enough to keep me from starving. They wanted me to be too weak to try an escape." Arnold spoke from the back seat. Christophe watched him in the rearview mirror. Cerbie seemed to have taken to him, and allowed Arnold to stroke him, which seemed to soothe the older man.

He looked like hell. Thin, feeble, weak, and dirty. And they couldn't go home. He couldn't even get into the bathrooms, because the sinks were broken, and their toiletries smeared all over the floors and walls. The glass wall in Arnold's bathroom had been smashed with a hammer. "You have nothing to apologize for, Arnold. It wasn't your fault. The Vampire Council was using you as a fulcrum to force me to..." He glanced at Zaira. "...do something for them. But they didn't show up to let me know they had you for nearly a month. The two vampires who took you...they've damaged the house. So we'll have to go somewhere else to stay for a few days."

"I hope you haven't done it, sir. Whatever they wanted you to do." There was vindictive anger in his voice.

"No, I haven't done it. And I won't. They've gone too far this time." He felt a wild rage every time he looked at Arnold. The man's cheeks were hollowed, his eyes sunken from not getting the proper nutrition. His wrists and ankles were swollen and raw. "I'm going to take you to..."

Zaira broke in. "Take him to my house. I have a spare bedroom there, and I've set wards against anyone who isn't invited in, vampire and witch alike. He can take a shower, and I'll fix him something to eat while you go out to buy him some clothes."

Christophe glanced in her direction. "Are you sure?"

"Yes. We'll be fine while you do what needs to be done."

"We have insurance on the house and the contents, sir. You need to contact an agent with the company and have them come out and look at the damage."

He didn't want to tell him how bad it was. Arnold prided himself on keeping the house clean and organized. For him to walk back into the place the way it was now and see everything destroyed...

"All the important papers are in your safety deposit box

at the bank."

"I'll go by after I drop you both off and take care of it." He didn't even have a key to the box. It was probably somewhere amid all the debris.

Zaira's house was the size of a postage stamp. He felt like a giant in the land of the Lilliputians standing in the living room. Zaira found Arnold some sweat pants and a T-shirt her brother left behind after a visit.

"I can't thank you enough for all you've done. I am grateful for you keeping him safe until I can get him some things."

"You're more upset for him than for yourself about the house."

"Yes. The house has always been more for him than me. He's going to be hurt by the loss." He shook his head. "He had a collection of antique snuff boxes. They're gone now."

"My offer still stands. I might be able to fix some things." She stepped close to him. "How long has he been with you?"

"A hundred years. He's been seeing one of the older ladies on our street, going to the movies, that kind of thing. She's called nearly every day since he's been gone. I told her he took a wildlife hike on the Appalachian trail with a friend for a month and was out of touch. If he wanted to take it further, I'd free him to do so. It's an antiquated practice, having a manservant these days. I'm not exactly helpless."

"Change is hard. And a hundred years is a long time."

It was. They might not be blood kin in the manner humans were, but they might as well be. "I'll be back as soon as I can."

"You have a lot to take care of. I can work from here until you get back."

He laid a hand on her shoulder. "Thank you." When they had time, he was going to show her how appreciative he was for all she'd done.

Her cheeks flared as though she'd read his mind and he smiled. "I'll be back as soon as I can."

The bank was helpful in helping him gain access to his bank account and safety deposit box, as was the police department. Armed with the insurance policy and a police report, he stopped by the insurance office and made an appointment.

Next he swung through a men's clothing store where he knew Arnold shopped and bought several pairs of pants and shirts for them both, as well as underwear, pajamas, and socks. He rushed through a discount department store and purchased toiletries, a couple of pairs of jeans for himself—Arnold wouldn't be caught dead in them—and pullover sweaters for each of them.

Three hours before he had to meet with the insurance adjuster, he returned to the house. The damage didn't look any better today than it had the evening before. He sifted through the ruins of Arnold's room to find what he could of the snuffboxes. Out of the fifteen he knew he had, he found twelve. Only two had survived intact, having been kicked beneath other debris. He hoped once he began to clean up, he'd find the other three.

The longer he surveyed the damage the angrier he became. When he saw the two vampires again, they would wish they hadn't set foot inside this house.

That thought brought two worrisome thoughts to the surface. First, Arnold's rescue had been too easy. Had they wanted to keep him longer, the witch they hired would have fought tooth and nail to keep him. They'd already gotten what they wanted from him, so they didn't need Arnold anymore. And the second: he needed to move the wand to a safer location. The safe had worked fine for the past few days, but he was beginning to feel antsy. The digital lock was foolproof against most humans, but not against magic. With sufficient power, they could rip the safe out of the floor and spring the door.

Now he had Arnold back he could destroy the damn thing.

More than satisfied with his plan, he rushed downstairs to his office, opened the safe, and extracted the wand, taking it into the garage where he stored the tools he used to fix the car and do small repairs around the house.

He got out heavy work gloves. The damn thing gave him the creeps every time he touched it, and he hoped the gloves would be thick enough to keep it from affecting him.

He opened the shipping tube and pulled the wand free of the towel. Its power penetrated the gloves immediately, and he grimaced. Fastening the piece of oak into the vise he used to hold metal parts in place, he lifted down a small handsaw from the pegboard over his work table. He'd cut the damn thing into pieces and burn it.

He rested the saw against the wand and, pressing down, he raked it back and forth, first lightly to get a start, then with greater force. The harder he pressed, down the more resistance he felt. He lifted the saw and stared in disbelief. The teeth of the instrument were tangled and flattened. There wasn't a mark on the wand.

There had to be some way to destroy the thrice-damned thing.

Half an hour later, the worktable was scattered with damaged tools. And he had a large knot on his forehead where the hammer he'd tried boomeranged back and hit him. The damn wand had a hell of a built-in defense mechanism.

He studied his reflection in one of his car's side view mirrors. It looked like he'd developed a zit between his eyes the size of an ostrich egg. It even had the red center, like it needed to be popped. If he had a gag reflex, it would be working overtime. And worse, it hurt like hell.

Surely the injury would heal before he returned to Zaira's house to collect Arnold.

He didn't bother to try the small acetylene torch. He didn't relish the idea of setting himself on fire.

If he couldn't destroy the fucking thing, he had to hide it

well enough so anyone who came looking would have to raze the house to find it.

He scanned the many tools he hadn't used yet and picked up a cordless drill, popping open the container of bits he had that fit the tool and selecting the biggest one. This would do.

He unscrewed the wand from the clamp and took it with him upstairs.

ZAIRA CLOSED THE bedroom door. Cerbie had taken up a watch next to Arnold, head on paws. She'd done some healing to ease the man's scrapes and bruises, so at least his wrists and ankles looked normal again.

Once Arnold had gotten some food and a shower, he'd dropped off to sleep as though someone had thrown a switch. He was completely exhausted, poor man. He'd needed to stay on guard against being attacked by both the vampires and the witch. He'd been reticent about his treatment, but she gathered from what he said that they'd threatened and tormented and tortured him, trying to get him to tell them every aspect of his master's life.

Master was such an antiquated term. After a hundred years together, they'd progressed beyond the servant-master relationship. She didn't feel that Chris was a master to the elderly man at all, but a loving nephew or son instead.

It was difficult, this relationship they built between preternatural being and human. Chris had the edge of being able to sustain Arnold's life through their connection. The vampire shared his energy through the bond. Had he not, Arnold might have succumbed to starvation or injury during his ordeal.

She'd volunteered her spare bedroom to ensure Chris didn't disappear now Arnold was safe. She needed more time to discover what the Vampire Council had demanded he do for them. If he was the thief who had stolen the wand, she needed to recover it from him and return it to the protection of the box and the storage facility.

But in the meantime, she needed to get some work done. She slipped into the bedroom again. Her voice just above a whisper, she said, "Keep an eye on Arnold for me, Cerbie."

His ears twitched. "I got this covered."

Stepping out into the hall, she teleported to Seymour Hurst's hotel in Lexington, Kentucky. He was visiting Transylvania College to encourage attendance at the next national WaVeS ball, which was for all preternatural creatures, but sponsored by the Witch, Vampire and Shifters' Councils. The concierge, who knew him from past conferences, pointed him out to her in the bar. The male witch was having a drink and chatting up a coed who looked a quarter of his age.

"Hello, Seymour," she greeted him as though they knew each other.

"Hello." He squinted his eyes as though nearsighted, not a good look for him, since, combined with his long, narrow nose and pointy chin, it emphasized his resemblance to an opossum. An opossum with spiked white hair.

"Could you spare me just five minutes? I was sent by your fellow Council members to ask you a few questions."

Seymour flushed red, and his white brows clamped together like they were bumping fists. He glanced around the room. "They're not here, are they?"

"No. Just me."

He breathed a relieved sigh.

The young woman sitting across from him rose and tossed blond ringlets over her shoulder. "I have another appointment, Seymour baby. We'll catch up before you leave to say good-bye." She leaned down and kissed his cheek.

Seymour baby? Zaira eyed the witch. Perhaps he was Mr. Personality Plus. That often offset an…um…unfortunate appearance.

He smiled, flashing large teeth in his narrow mouth. "How about two a.m., Laverne? I'll be in my room by then."

"That sounds good." She nodded to Zaira and strutted through the crowded bar.

He cupped his chin in his hand and followed the woman's progress across the room with rapt attention until she exited the bar. "You'd never know she's a hooker by looking at her, would you?"

Zaira's mouth flew open and she quickly closed it.

He motioned to the seat the girl had vacated. "Those tight-assed curmudgeons never let me have any fun. What have they sent you here for?"

Zaira bit her lip to keep from laughing. "Right after you left to come to Transylvania, a special artifact went missing from the Council storage facility."

His eyes widened. "No shit?"

Caught by surprise, Zaira laughed. "No shit."

He remained silent for a moment. "This artifact wouldn't by any chance come from Ireland, would it?"

"Yes, it would."

"Shit!"

He spoke so loudly several nearby patrons looked up.

He took a big gulp of the cocktail sitting in front of him.

Zaira leaned forward and placed her arms on the table.

"I had a feeling something like this might go down." He raked his hand over his spiked hair. "They were all sticking their noses in where they didn't belong. Councilwoman Nelson is away, and they've been spending their time going through things. I'm afraid some of them have delusions of grandeur."

"The only one I've had any dealings with is Glendora."

"Don't let that ditzy Marilyn Monroe impression fool you. Behind those boobs beats a heart of stone. Great boobs, though." He lost his train of thought, or maybe he was following it, then suddenly jerked his attention back to her. "I think she's got her eyes on the head Councilwoman's job, and she doesn't care how she gets it.

Zaira didn't know why anyone would want it. All that power would be great, but having to deal with witchy issues all the time, not so much.

"You wouldn't happen to know where Councilwoman Nelson is vacationing, would you? In case this turns into an emergency."

"No, I don't. And she wouldn't be happy if you contacted her, either. She hasn't had a vacation in at least a hundred years." He rested his elbow on the table, but it slipped off the edge, and he took a header toward the floor. His feet hovered in the air for a moment before he flipped back into his seat in a gymnastic mount that might have earned him a seat on team Witch.

Dear Goddess, he was hammered.

"I do know she's dating some romance novel cover model whose actually a witch."

Zaira sat up in shock. "I know who you're talking about? I thought he was gay?"

"Who knows?" He chuckled and waved a hand. "If I was looking for her, I'd start with the Bahamas. The last romance novel cover he did was there."

Zaira rose. "Thank you. I appreciate your help."

"And there's one more thing." Seymour weaved in his seat and his words were beginning to slur. "The artifact we're talking about…It's damn dan—" he belched "—gerous."

Then his forehead hit the tabletop with a thump. He'd passed out, thank the Goddess.

Chapter 7

AFTER MAKING SURE Seymour was taken to his motel room, Zaira popped back home, checked on Arnold, and settled on the couch with her laptop to do some research, and wasn't surprised when she found very little of anything to do with the wand. She'd have to turn to other resources for that.

Hearing Seymour Hurst expounding on the dangers of the device didn't exactly clue her in on exactly how dangerous.

She turned her attention to the Sutherlands. He owned a huge construction company specializing in office buildings, apartment complexes, and other structures. Of late they had lost a few bids, and business had fallen off. And when she looked up his county and city taxes, she learned his tax payments had been late for the past two years.

She moved on to public records, where she found two lawsuits filed. His company was being sued for failure to finish one structure, and for never starting another.

After a little finessing, she brought up their financial information, and saw they were nearly broke. That three hundred thousand was going to come in handy.

Next she researched Chris. It hadn't occurred to Arnold to be anything but forthcoming with information. When she looked up Christophe Bakas, she learned he had degrees in American and European History, and a doctorate in Political Science. He had taught at the community college for ten years. He had no property in his name other than his car. The house must be in Arnold's. She tried Arnold Bakas and came up empty. She hadn't thought to ask him his full name.

A car pulled up in the driveway, and she closed the laptop and went to the door. Chris looked like he'd been mucking around in a barnyard, but smelled like he'd been sprayed with soap. His shoes were smeared with...was that shampoo? With a wave of her hand, she cleaned his clothing and shoes before he stepped into the house. He dropped a large collection of bags beside the door.

"Thanks, the shoes are the only pair I have. I didn't have time to shop for more. How's he doing?"

"He's sleeping. Cerbie's with him, on guard. I think he must have been under duress the entire time he was held."

"I'm sure he was."

Of course, he'd feel the draw of energy from him whenever something happened to Arnold.

He pulled several oddly-shaped things from both pockets of his jacket. "I was hoping you could do something with these."

When she realized what they were, quick tears pricked

her eyes. She'd had several vampire clients, had felt their emotions and their lack of them. Chris was an oddity. Touched by his gesture, she placed the boxes on the coffee table and sat down in front of them. She picked each one up to study, trying to get an idea of how it looked before it was damaged. Then she touched each one, fixing it as she went. He added two more to the group that seemed to have survived unscathed.

"There were three missing. I'll look again when I start cleaning up the mess."

"I'm sure Arnold will appreciate it." She said her voice husky with emotion. "You look like you could use something to drink."

"Yes, I could. You healed him, didn't you?"

"Yes."

"I felt your energy." His pale gray eyes took on the silver glow, and his throat worked as he swallowed. He brushed his hand down her arm, raising the tiny hairs there against his palm.

Her heart fluttered like bat wings at her throat and wrists, not from the fear she should have been feeling, but the power of her need. His touch was like static electricity playing upon her nerve endings, bringing them to life. She swayed toward him, craving more. His beard brushed her temple as he drew her close. He felt solid, muscular, and manly. Very manly. And his response to her pushed against her stomach.

"If we made love, we'd share power the way we're doing right now." His hand splayed against her spine, molding her closer.

Oh Goddess! The cautious voice inside her shouting, *no falling for a vampire* was drowned out by the hungry beat of her heart.

"It's very pleasurable. And I promise not to bite." He nibbled her ear.

She felt a heartbeat throbbing against her palm just as fast as her own and wondered at it. He nibbled her neck and she went hot, wet, and tingling in seconds. She slipped her arms around his neck and pressed closer. They rocked against each other. At Chris's husky groan, sensual chills rushed across her skin.

His lips found hers. He'd had over two hundred years to perfect his kissing technique, and Zaira thanked the Goddess for every day of it. His soft, sweet kisses built to passionate consummation of teeth and tongue that both terrified and thrilled her. She rode the razor-sharp edge of need as his tongue tempted and teased her own into a hungry, sensual battle that pushed her to the brink.

And when he lifted her and pressed her back against the door, fitting himself against her in just the right spot, she wrapped her legs around his waist and welcomed the pressure against her hyper-sensitive core. With two rolling thrusts of his hips he brought her to completion. The power of her orgasm rolled over her, through her like a tsunami, and she felt it spread over him, through him, until his release throbbed against her. They were both gasping.

"Imagine how much better it would have been if I'd been inside you, Zaira."

If it got any better, she might not survive.

He kissed her softly and set her gently on her feet.

Oh, Goddess, what had she done? He was a client, and she'd just crossed the line, something she'd never done before.

He excused himself and went down the hall to clean up.

As soon as he was out of sight, she began to pace the floor, berating herself. She'd never allowed anyone to get so close to her so quickly. She'd completely dropped her defenses because of the care he showed to Arnold. Every time she moved she felt her damp panties and relived that final moment. How much better could it have been if he'd been inside her?

She was not falling for him. No matter how good he was at sharing power.

She didn't like the panicked feeling of guilt and confusion that tumbled inside her.

She slipped down the hall to her room, wiggled free of her panties, and slipped on a fresh pair.

She exited her room at the same time he exited the bathroom. He caught her guilty flush and smiled. His silver-gray eyes delved into hers. "Don't regret a moment of it. I'm not going to." He kissed her again.

"You're a client, Chris. There are rules."

"Not anymore, Zaira. You saved Arnold. Now it will be up to me to see him safe." He reached inside the interior jacket pocket and withdrew an envelope of money. "This is the fee we settled on for your services." He offered it to her.

She wrapped her fingers around the envelope. "Where will you and he go?"

"I was hoping you would allow Arnold to stay the night while I clean up the house. I'm going to encourage him and his lady take a cruise together until I take care of this…issue."

"That might be a good idea."

"And while he's gone, I'll have the house repaired."

"It may take a little time to get things done."

Christophe raised a brow. "I can be very persuasive."

She could attest to that. She'd barely known what hit her.

She was developing a soft spot for this handsome vampire cat burglar. And a passion for him.

She couldn't afford a vampire in her life. There was too much prejudice against vampire-witch couples in the preternatural community. It would destroy her business.

And there was still the question of the wand.

With clearer thoughts came guilt. She had kissed him. They'd shared power. And she was thinking about how she could use him to get the wand back.

He laid a fingertip against her bottom lip, his full attention focused there. He kissed her again, and her chaotic thoughts took a hike as though there was a switch that turned off her brain as soon as his lips touched hers.

She had to do something about that.

"I've been wondering about something. Did you see the witch who was guarding Arnold?"

"No, but he gave me a description. She was older, with dark hair and eyes. But then she could have been using a disguise spell."

"His rescue was too easy. There has to be a reason why they allowed us to take him."

She had thought the same thing. And she had the edgy feeling she always got when something wasn't quite right.

"When do you want me to meet with the Sutherlands?"

She'd almost decided against it. "I looked into their finances. You were right. They're up to their eyebrows in debt."

He nodded. "I can give them back the money I got for the gems. Now I have Arnold back, I no longer need it."

"There wouldn't be much point in that. Send it to the insurance company instead. They're going to be paying it out, unless I turn the Sutherlands in. But I don't have any proof they're defrauding the company. Or no proof I can give the company without turning you in."

"I have put you in a difficult position." Regret tempered his expression.

"There is one thing you could do for me."

"Anything."

"Tell me what the Vampire Council asked you to do."

He remained silent for a long moment. "They asked me to use my skills to steal something and bring it to them."

Yes! She knew it. "And did you?"

"No. We've been at an impasse, because I didn't trust them to return Arnold. I don't trust them not to try to take him again, either. It has been my experience they will do whatever it takes to further their agendas, and to hell with everyone else."

At an impasse about stealing it or giving it to them? He didn't distinguish between the two. It sounded very much like how she'd felt about the Magic Council in the past. But Adira Nelson did things a little differently. She didn't put up with any shit.

"Adcock is a dick."

Hearing him use slang without his formal speech always surprised her. She laughed.

He grinned, mirroring her amusement, and her heart turned over. He was way too attractive, and with his kindness to Arnold...

"But he's a very powerful dick. If I do what he wants, he can turn me into the Council for stealing something dangerous to vampires. Then they can burn me or stake me without a trial."

He had the wand. She knew it. "So you're stuck between a rock and a hard place."

"Yes, you could say that."

She'd be saving his life if she could find the wand and steal it from him. It might at least assuage some of her guilt over using him to get it.

"Let me come to your house with you. After the insurance adjuster has a chance to evaluate the damage, I can help you clean up." And she could search for the wand. If it was on the premises, she'd be able to feel its power. She decided to follow him, whether he took her with him or not.

Chris studied her for a long moment. "Once you know who I am, where I live...."

"If I turned you in now, I'd be considered an accomplice. You've just given me money."

He nodded. "What about Arnold?"

"Cerbie is guarding him. But I'll call Calamity and ask her to come over."

"Calamity?"

"Our receptionist at work."

"What's her middle name?"

"Jane."

"Can she shoot?"

"If you ask her that, she might give you a painful demonstration."

Chapter 8

S HE HAD NEVER seen a vampire barbecue before. She'd always believed they were afraid of fire. Chris turned to get another package of burgers to put on the grill, and she glimpsed the front of his apron. A small red devil decorated the top corner of the apron, and below it read HOT STUFF.

She laughed aloud, but agreed with the assessment. In fact, when she stepped out the back door onto the patio, she checked out his jeans-covered ass, and damn if that part of his anatomy didn't look as good as the rest of him.

"Hey, Hot Stuff. Nice apron," she greeted him.

He grinned. "One of the girls bought it when I sent them to the market for food."

She laughed. "I bet they all flirt with you and compete for your attention."

"They're too young for me." He dropped his deep voice to a rumble. "And too human."

"That makes for a lonely existence, Christophe, when they're the dominant species. Don't most men take their opportunities where they find them?"

"When you have an eternity to live, lonely is a relative

term. I've been married to two humans, and I've had to bury them both. I avoid them now."

Something in his face gripped her throat with emotion.

"You smell delicious." He leaned over to nuzzle her neck. His silver eyes gleamed, the look in their depths arrowing straight to intimate areas of her anatomy and in an instant she was wet with need. He ran a hand down her spine. If she leaned into him, they'd be ripping each other's clothes off right in front of the grill and light a fire much hotter than the lava rock.

A crash inside drew their attention and reminded her of the students. "I'd better go check on that."

"Maybe so," his voice sounded husky, and his expression held regret.

The sound of young people's voices carried through the house as she climbed the stairs. The group of ten students had shown up at his door at eight o'clock, just as she was leaving for home to take a much-needed shower.

Unlike vampires, witches sweated just like regular people. She and Chris had worked almost all night and gotten most of the downstairs cleaned up. And now the students worked on the bedrooms upstairs.

With one wave of a hand, she could have done it all, but there was a price each time she did magic. It borrowed from something in the environment, and the cost was cumulative. So for her to use magic it needed to really matter.

"Need some help?" she asked as she poked her head into

one of the bedrooms, where five of them had congregated with garbage bags and shovels.

"Naw." The red-headed young man she'd seen at the diner, Andy, answered. "This box spring seems to have survived intact. We'll prop it over in the corner. Professor B will only need a mattress here." He frowned. "Well, and a new bed." The frame of the cherrywood bed was hacked to pieces.

"I'm sure he'll be pleased to know something survived."

One of the girls approached her. "We found pieces of a photo scattered on the bed. I've saved them in case they were important to him."

"Thank you." She cupped her hands to take them from the young blonde.

"I hope they find who did this. Professor Bakas is a good guy. If they were determined to wipe out any proof he'd lived in this house, they did a excellent job of it."

Goosebumps trailed over Zaira's skin. "I'll see what I can do with these. Keep an eye out for more."

"Will do."

She made one more pass through the bedrooms, searching for the wand. She sensed no power, but then until the power was called upon, it might not give off a power signature.

She needed to bring the box to the house and see if it continued to call to the wand. It might guide her to it.

She waited until she was downstairs in the kitchen alone

before she waved a hand over the pieces of photograph. They rose in the air, shuffled themselves and settled back down on the counter. The bottom left corner was missing, but the important parts were there. It was a picture of a woman. A very beautiful woman. The lace day gown left her shoulders bare, while a bustle accentuated her hourglass shape. She looked over her shoulder at the camera. Her skin glowed flawless and pale against the dark hair hanging in elaborate curls to her waist.

Chris came in from the back patio with a pan of well-cooked hamburgers. He set them on the counter and wandered over to see what she was looking at.

"You found Lynette."

"One of the girls found the pieces upstairs. I think her name is Brittany."

"I'll have to thank her. This is the only image I have of my second wife. I thought it was lost."

She ignored the twinge she felt at the word wife. The woman was dead. She had no reason to feel jealous of her. She was no competition.

Whoa! Where did that thought come from?

She dragged her mind away from her reaction to something that bothered her more. "Do you think they're trying to wipe out every trace of you here?"

His gaze leapt to hers and the gray darkened to pewter. "Yes. Probably so."

She read no fear in his gaze.

How could he be so calm? The Vampire Council had to know he had the wand. They had just tried unsuccessfully to find it themselves. She had to talk him into giving it to her. It might save his life.

A knock came at the front door. "I'll get that. I'm expecting some contractors and the insurance adjuster." She heard him yell up to the students, telling them their food was ready.

She waved a hand over the photo and fit the pieces together into a single whole, then slipped the photo into the empty pantry. The students would find it strange if they discovered the ruined photo had suddenly become whole.

He returned to the kitchen with a check as the students wandered in.

Zaira caught a glimpse of the amount printed on it. "You really are persuasive, aren't you?"

"The insurance has been in place for fifty years without a single claim. I brought that up while we were talking."

"No vampire woo-woo?"

He chuckled. "No. No vampire woo-woo. I'm very selective about when, where, and with whom I share my woo-woo." He looped an arm around her waist and drew her in close. He smelled like outdoors, the grill, and lemon-scented soap. He'd pushed the sleeves of his blue pullover sweater up to his elbows, exposing well-shaped forearms and banding the muscles in his upper arms. The sweater hugged his chest, outlining his pectoral muscles. Chest hair lay visible above the V-neckline of the sweater.

She loved a man with chest hair. Not a mat like a shedding horse, but just enough to emphasize his virility. As though Chris needed that.

She looked around the kitchen at the students stuffing their mouths with burgers and potato salad, and noticed their interest in the interaction between them. Goddess, they'd caught her checking him out. Color heated her cheeks, and she turned to lean back against the counter.

"I need to go. I have work to do."

"What about the Sutherlands?"

She drew him out of the kitchen onto the patio and closed the door. "I've contacted them and told them I found their burglar, but that you were very cagey about meeting them. I suggested a video chat might work. That way they can't get too close. I can make a charm that will disguise your appearance for a short time.

"That sounds interesting."

"This is a suggestion. You may want to practice a different accent or dumb down your diction. As it is, the way you speak is very distinctive."

He grinned. "I think I can manage that."

They set up a time. Chris walked her back through the kitchen to the front door. Zaira turned to say good-bye and looked past his shoulder to find the students peering around the edge of the door, watching them.

"Your students have taken a real interest in what's going

on between us."

"They've been paying into a pool all semester about whether I'm gay or straight, was in a relationship, or was grieving a loss. I think there were several other options to bet on. They even speculated that Arnold and I were involved." He raised a brow at that. He ran his hand down the long tail of hair that hung over her shoulder. "You wouldn't want to help me lay all that to rest, would you?"

"I wouldn't have thought any of that would bother you."

"It doesn't. As long as they're looking for mundane things, my real secrets are safe. But I am angling for a good-bye kiss." He gripped the end of her braided ponytail and wrapped it around his hand. "When I saw you on that roof, I had visions of doing this and exposing your lovely neck so I could drink from you. Does that idea disturb you?

Zaira's mouth went bone-dry, and she was tingling and wet again. "A little," her voice came out a little squeaky.

He smiled. "I'll give you some time to think about it. It can be very erotic." He eased in close and, giving her hair a tug to tilt her chin up and cupping the back of her head, lowered his lips to hers in a slow, thorough, sensual kiss she felt from her lips to the aching juncture between her legs, and maybe even all the way to her toes. When he finally broke the kiss and lifted his head, it took her a moment to open her eyes.

"You're very good at that," she managed.

"That isn't all, Zaira."

Oh, my Goddess. She walked all the way to her car before she could draw breath enough to even remind herself sternly that *she was not falling for a vampire. No matter how good a kisser he was.*

Chapter 9

THE BEATING AND banging going on inside the house while repairs were being completed drove Christophe from the house to the library to work. But the quiet there burrowed under his skin like chiggers, leaving him itchy.

Now Arnold and his lady friend were safely aboard the cruise ship, under a cloaking spell so they couldn't be found, and out of harm's way, he'd expected the Council to descend upon him, but they hadn't.

There had to be a reason why they hadn't made a move yet. He spent his time preparing for when they did.

The video chat earlier in the day with the Sutherlands had gone well. Wearing the disguise charm had been strangely entertaining. He'd become the rather rough speaking, less educated burglar Zaira's charm had created. Lorraine and Maxwell had been sincerely grateful for his warning about their daughter's heart. Maxwell Sutherland had even hinted at a monetary reward for keeping things between them. He'd been a little suspicious about Chris's "Naw, dude. We're good." Until he'd explained he'd been a parent too.

The experience had stirred feelings in him he tried to bury. Pain he did his best to shut out. His children were gone, as were his wives. He probably had a number of descendants, but to introduce himself to them now would require too much explanation and only disrupt their lives. No human needed a vampire in their family directing the Vampire Council's interest to them. To them humans were food, or a convenience, not something or someone you cared about.

And that brought him back to what had been bothering him ever since the video chat with the Sutherlands. He needed to break it off with Zaira. Every time they met, he could be putting her in danger.

But he just couldn't do it. It had been 1912 when last he'd felt this way about a woman. The Goddess only knew when he'd feel this way again.

And it wasn't as if she were a defenseless human. She had skills.

But if anything should happen to her….

He raked his fingers through his hair, pushing the curls back from his forehead. Too restless to continue reading the book, he shut it and rose. He had several contacts he'd emailed for information about magical siphons, and how to control them. He'd wait and see what came in. He returned the books to the shelves, closed his new laptop, and pushed it into his backpack.

The early summer sun was bright, and he flinched from

its touch. Though he could withstand it, it took energy, for his body was in a constant state of healing itself every second he was exposed to its rays. He didn't know how humans bore it. He shoved sunglasses on his face and strode swiftly to his car.

Once inside the vehicle, he put the backpack in the passenger seat and breathed a sigh of relief. Maybe a drive would clear his mind and help him resign himself to the necessity of putting some distance between him and Zaira. It would be in her best interest. She didn't need to get dragged into vampire politics. Especially with witches involved, too.

He started the car and pulled out onto the quiet street, meandering down Main and crossing over to Magic.

They hadn't taken that last step into consummating their relationship. Hearts weren't involved yet, just libidos. She continued to hold him at arm's length, though he knew she wanted him. For every hundred questions she asked, she answered one. Which didn't exactly encourage the building of a relationship. It spoke of a lack of trust, and without trust how could they move on to other things?

But for the first time in a very long time he was tempted to want a real bond. She was a witch, not a human. They could have hundreds of years together. But was he thinking with his libido instead of his head? Their power was a perfect match. It made him wonder how well they'd match in other ways.

Would he get an opportunity to find out?

He took the entrance ramp to the mountain pass. He hit the gas, and the Aston Martin went into takeoff mode. The vehicle had a speedometer that climbed to a hundred and forty-five miles and hour. He'd only had it up to a hundred-twenty once or twice. Now the car had a little age on it—it was, after all, more than fifty years old—he didn't want to push it too hard.

Seeing a large black SUV gaining on him in his rear view mirror, he shifted gears and let the engine breathe a little more. The road branched out into four lanes, two going north, two going south. Expecting the larger car to pull around, he stayed in the slow lane, going eighty.

The chrome grill at the front of the SUV grew larger in his rearview mirror. He sped up a little more. The larger vehicle kept pace, even though it was heavier. With a sudden burst of speed it rushed up and bumped him from behind.

It had to be the Council. He controlled the car's swerve from side to side until it gripped the road again.

He shoved the gas pedal to the floor. The fifty-year-old engine growled deep and shot forward, the speedometer rushing up to one hundred twenty. The SUV did the same. They hit a long, deep curve that slingshotted around the mountain. While the smaller car hugged the inside of the curve, the larger swung out beside him and edged over. The passenger door of the SUV filled his vision as it crept close. The windows were tinted, but he could still see the large man behind the window. Christophe gripped the steering wheel hard. A crash would only kill him if the car burned. But he'd need time to heal before they were on him.

The window rolled down and the barrel of a sawed-off shotgun thrust out. "Pull over."

He heard the bellow over the revving of both engines. Not witches or vampires, but shifters. Christophe stomped on the brakes, burning rubber as the wheels locked. The SUV shot forward and swerved sideways as it came to a stop in the center of the road.

Christophe ripped away the seatbelt and was out of the vehicle before they ever got their doors open. Fangs bared, claws distended, he leapt and landed atop the roof of the vehicle. The blast of the shotgun going off inside the cab echoed across the mountains and opened the roof of the SUV where he was standing.

Some of the pellets struck his shoulder and burned like a blowtorch. He leapt down, reached through the window, grabbed the shifter on the passenger side by the head, and jerked him through the window. He hammered his head against the SUV's door, creating a dent, dropped the unconscious shifter on the ground and started to circle the SUV in search of the other one.

A voice spoke from the other side of the vehicle. "The Vampire Council just wants to meet with you. We were sent to pick you up."

"Yes. Like I'm going to get into a vehicle with shifters

armed with sawed-off shotguns. You shouldn't have come armed, asshole. Have you never heard of a cell phone, a letter, an email, or a telegram? Tell the Council if they want to meet with me, to ring my fucking doorbell like civilized beings instead of sending their goons to kidnap or injure me."

He jerked free a piece of the shrapnel sticking out of his shoulder. It pinged as it struck the ground at his feet. Blood splattered his new shoes. His rage climbed higher. He picked up the limp, unconscious shifter at the side of the SUV and crammed him back through the window.

He caught a glimpse of the driver of the SUV, who was partially shifted, his wolf eyes glowing, his claws distended.

"Begone, before I rip your fucking head off and punt it like a soccer ball."

THE WORKMEN'S VOICES carried to her as Zaira tiptoed down the hall into the mudroom and laundry at the back of the house. She cushioned her footsteps with magic so the workers wouldn't hear her, but decided she couldn't do a cloaking spell for fear of interfering with the connection between the box and the wand. She expected to see a change in the symbols' movements once the container and wand were reunited, but thus far nothing had changed.

Once in the office, she searched every space, but left the new desk for last. As soon as she approached it, the symbols on the box went into hyperdrive. She pointed it at the top drawers, but calligraphic carvings neither increased nor decreased their gyrations. She methodically pointed the box at each drawer. When she set the box down on the floor to look through the bottom drawers, the symbols practically danced off the surface of the container.

Could he have put the wand under the floor? She rolled back the carpet and ran her hands over the hard wood. It took some moments, but she found a section of flooring that popped up. When she discovered the safe, her excitement peaked, flushing her cheeks with heat. It couldn't be that easy.

The digital lock was hardly a challenge for her magic. She opened the container and found only a document covered in a plastic sleeve. It was similar to the one the Witch Council gave her, but this one looked authentic, and had a great deal more information about the wand. After reading the sheet she sat stunned, her heart pounding at her throat and wrists. Fear settled with the weight of a crystal ball somewhere between her stomach and her heart. The thing was far more dangerous than she'd ever suspected, and she'd suspected plenty.

Where was the wand? Obviously somewhere else in the house, because it wasn't with the document. Wherever it was, it needed to be destroyed. She climbed the stairs to the bedrooms. Two workers came out of the main bathroom balancing a large sheet of broken glass that had been the shower door between them.

They both came to a halt and stared at her.

They'd already seen her. It was too late for her to do a cloaking spell. She'd just have to play it out. "Hi. I'm just leaving a gift for Professor Bakus." She lifted the box.

"He isn't here. I think he went to the library."

"I'll just leave it in his bedroom."

One of the guys grinned, a knowing light in his eye that irritated her. "Sure." They continued down the stairs with the broken sheet of glass.

She wandered around two of the bedrooms with no reaction. When she reached the third bedroom, the only one with room-darkening shutters, the symbols on the box went wild. She slipped inside and closed the door.

The room smelled like Chris. The faint fragrance of citrus and soap lingered in the air. It was a masculine room, with dark walnut furnishings and navy blue curtains with taupe-colored valances matching the comforter and bedding. Clear glass lamps graced the tables flanking the bed on each side, and a beautifully textured grasscloth covered the wall behind the headboard.

The room suited Chris, the lack of clutter reminding her of the recent loss of all his belongings. A sudden rush of regret nearly sent her back out the door.

She'd signed a contract with the Council promising to return the wand. She had to do this.

But to betray his trust was killing her. If she did this, they could never exchange power again. He'd never forgive her. Tears threatened, and an ache swamped her.

She stood for a long moment in the center of the space, fighting her conscience and her emotions.

She had a reputation to protect. She always found the missing person, object, document, book. Whatever she searched for. She never failed. Even if it hurt. She had a business to protect. She had employees who depended on her. Depended on the living they made working for her.

All those arguments were legitimate. But it didn't ease the ache.

She sighed and straightened her shoulders and moved slowly around the perimeter of the room. She opened each drawer, wondering what could be holding the wand back if it were here. Maybe it wasn't and she could forget all this. She might even relish being wrong about him having the wand.

A strange tapping sound came from somewhere close to the bed, and she approached the area cautiously. Any time magic was involved, anything could happen. A piece of the grasscloth close to the corner of the room seemed to have something beneath it that caused a faint protrusion, like the head of an eraser was pressing out from beneath it.

She set the box on the bed and stretched out a hand, palm up. A razor appeared in her grasp. She carefully made a small slit in the expensive wall covering. A sharp piece of wood corkscrewed from a hole drilled into the wall, at first slowly, then with greater and greater speed. With a sudden shudder, it slid free of its hiding space and shot, arrow-fast, past her head.

Goddess! That was close! So close she'd felt the air disturbed by its passage brush her cheek.

She turned to find the box sitting quietly on the bed. The symbols were finally stationary. She raised the lid and found the wand nestled in the interior.

She was doing the right thing. With it gone, the Vampire Council couldn't stake or burn Chris for stealing it. There would be no evidence he'd ever had it.

She shook her head, knowing she was trying to find a way to rationalize her behavior and make what she was doing right. They were both stuck in untenable situations. But his life was more important than this wand. Couldn't he see that?

She picked up the box on the bed, tucked it under her arm. Her cell phone vibrated in her pocket and she tugged it free. At the sight of Chris's number she debated whether or not to answer it. This might be the last time they spoke. She couldn't bring herself to ignore the call.

"I'm in need of a healer. Can you meet me at the house?"

She looked around the room and her skin burned with guilt. Fear zoomed right past the emotion, setting her heart to flying and making her breathing erratic. "What's happened?"

"The Council sent shifters to bring me in for a meeting. We had a slight confrontation. I have a couple of small pieces of shrapnel lodged in my shoulder and can't get them out. If I don't remove them quickly, my body will heal around them.

"I'll be h-there waiting for you."

Chapter 10

C HRIS PULLED THE car into the garage and turned off the engine. His shoulder and arm still burned from the injury, and he reached across to open the door with his left hand. It swung open before he could touch the handle.

Zaira looked pale, and her hazel eyes widened with concern as she took in his bloody clothing.

"Some of it isn't mine." He didn't know if that sounded reassuring or not.

She backed away, allowing him to exit the car. He unbuttoned his shirt and peeled the bloody sleeve away from his shoulder, wadding the ruined garment into a ball and tossing it in a large trashcan next to his worktable.

Taking off his T-shirt took less finesse. He just ripped it free and tossed it in the can, too.

Zaira approached him. She waved away the blood on his pants and shoes, lifting it in the air and tossing it in with the ruined shirts. She turned her attention to the open holes in his shoulder.

"It's buckshot from a shotgun blast."

She held her hand over his shoulder about two inches

from the injury and closed her eyes.

Without the adrenaline racing through his system to numb the process, pulling the bits of metal from his body hurt more than they had going in. He gritted his teeth and tried to remind himself to breathe, though it wasn't a natural thing anymore. Because the wounds had partially healed, some of them were already covered over. Blood poured down his arm as the buckshot popped free of his skin. A piece of blue metal a little bigger than his thumb came out as well. The injuries closed and were gone in seconds.

Zaira swayed and put a hand on the worktable to steady herself.

Chris caught her with his good arm.

"It'll pass in a minute." Her skin was white, and she sucked in a cleansing breath.

"I'm sorry, Zaira. I didn't realize…"

"There's always a price to pay. It's the way of it." She banished the blood on his arm to the trashcan, then ran a soothing hand over his shoulder. "How does it feel?"

"Fine, better." He rotated it to prove it. He drew her close to hold her. She smelled like magic and cinnamon, the scent of her blood just beneath the surface. The sound of her heart beat loud in his ears. It seemed to thrum beneath his skin, against the bones of his face. He wanted, needed to take her into him. Needed to be inside her. The idea aroused him to the point of pain.

He nuzzled her ear, then her neck.

✧ ✧ ✧

ZAIRA RAKED HER fingers through his hair. Power poured off him. She could feel his hunger, and her heart raced to meet it.

Once he found out what she'd done, she'd never know what it was to be held and kissed by him again. Never know what they could share. Unless she gave into this now.

She turned her head to kiss him and nicked the tip of her tongue on his fang. Chris groaned and kissed her, sucking on the tip and drawing it into his mouth. The cut was inconsequential amidst the sensations he inspired in the intimate areas of her body. Her breasts felt hot and full, a tingly shiver of excitement worked its way down her body and she grew wet. The need for him to touch her, fill her, left her aching.

He broke the kiss, and she realized the cut was healed.

"Are the repairmen still inside?" he asked.

"Yes." She snapped her fingers and they were suddenly in Chris's bedroom, the door closed.

"Handy trick, that." His eyes were glowing silver, but he'd retracted his fangs. "I have a few tricks of my own." She suddenly found herself lying in the center of the bed, her clothes gone. All she'd felt was a brush of air against her skin. He was completely nude in the blink of an eye. Wide-shouldered and slender-hipped, he glided to the bed on long legs as well developed as the rest of him. His stomach rippled with muscles as he stretched out beside her. His erection had expanded and lengthened.

His power brushed against her, and the fine hairs on her arms lifted toward him. It was like a caress rushing over her skin without his even having to touch her. When he kissed her, she shut off the voice in her head screeching this was a mistake. Because she wanted and cared about this vampire. When he found out what she had done, he was going to be furious, but until then, they were in sync with each other.

She allowed her power to flow to him and slid her arms around him, holding him close. She opened the empathic line between them and felt his passion blend with hers, felt the emotion behind it and her eyes glazed with tears. She was more than a hundred years old, and had never experienced such emotion from a lover.

He was a master at making love. She hadn't expected his tenderness, his care. Every caress, every kiss, built her need. She tried to build his in return. When he finally took her she cried out in pleasure.

In the throes of her orgasm, he struck and drank from her. Another wave of pleasure rolled over her, more intense than before, and triggered his release.

They both lay still, their bodies remaining linked.

"Do you sleep?" she asked as her hands ran up and down his back.

"I sleep like the dead about three hours a night."

"Don't tease about that." He was more alive than most of the male witches she'd met. Most of the humans as well.

His gray gaze grew thoughtful.

"You could have been killed today." She cupped his face then smoothed back the ridiculously sexy curls from his temple.

"Not likely, but possibly."

"Over what?"

"Over a group of vampires who are still living in the dark ages and who refuse to adapt enough to pick up a phone. That's why I was injured. But it would have taken more than a bit of metal to kill me."

She shook her head and twined her arms about his neck. "Are you going to pick up a phone and call them?"

"I would if they had a cell phone or land line. If they want to talk, they're going to have to come to the house and knock on the door or ring the doorbell, just like every other civilized species on the planet."

"Was that the message you sent back to them?"

"Yes."

"And what are you going to do when they show up at your door asking if you've stolen what they were looking for?"

Her cell phone rang and they looked at each other. She levitated it from the floor to her hand and brushed her thumb over the screen to answer the call.

Calamity sounded breathless. "Glendora Ghostly, the assistant to the Councilwoman, is here for an update."

Shit! She looked up into Chris's eyes and bit her lip. "I'll be right there." She closed out the call. "I have to go."

"Are you sure?"

He kissed her, and for a moment, with his lips and tongue coaxing hers into playful, sensual action, she forgot about everything but how it felt to have him moving inside her. She groaned. "I don't want to, but this is an extremely important and difficult client, and I have to meet with her."

He sighed. "Will you come back after the meeting?"

"I don't know. That depends on what happens during and after the meeting." She wasn't lying about that. "But I'll call you either way." She was going to hear a great deal from him as soon as he discovered the wand was gone. He'd put two and two together pretty quickly. Guilt twisted her stomach like a pretzel.

"Okay." He eased away from her, his reluctance obvious, and rolled aside to allow her to get up.

Still keyed into his emotions, she felt his disappointment.

She took her time getting dressed, enjoying the way his eyes followed her as she put on her bra and panties. By the time she stepped into her skirt and blouse she was enjoying the view of his response to the reverse striptease.

She paused to lean over him, cupped his cheek, and kissed him. Her composure wavered, and she blinked against the sting of tears and quickly turned away."

"I'll call you." She didn't give him time to respond before she teleported out.

Chapter 11

CHRISTOPHE STRETCHED AND lay back against the pillows, reliving every moment of their lovemaking. Making love with Zaira was as hot as he had imagined it. And she had allowed him to drink from her.

The weakness he'd experienced beforehand had passed. He felt strong and himself. But there was something missing besides his clothes. Something niggled on the edge of his consciousness. He was lying naked on the bed. With repairmen working in the house. He sat up and swung his legs over the side of the bed and it struck him.

The constant humming he'd been trying to block out for the past two days had gone silent.

He rushed to the corner of the room and touched the grasscloth. He felt the hole he'd drilled, and his finger parted the wall covering too easily. Someone had cut it. The empty hole stared back at him.

Fuck! Someone had taken the wand. He dressed in a nanosecond and raced down the hall to where the repairmen were still beating and banging.

He popped into the room and stood at the door, observing for a moment as they manhandled a heavy sheet of glass back into place to block off the shower and act as the door. He waited impatiently until they stabilized it before asking, "Did anyone come by today while I was gone?"

He suspected whom, but it still stung to hear one man say. "That pretty redhead who's been around for the last few days. She brought you something and left it in your room."

"Thanks."

He paced back and forth in the hall as anger climbed into his throat and attempted to strangle him. She had made love with him, and the entire time she was covering up that she had stolen the wand. She'd betrayed him!

How the hell had she found it?

What about the phone call and her immediate response? What if she was returning the wand to the Council right now?

He rushed down the stairs and out the front door.

✧　✧　✧

THANK THE GODDESS she had teleported the wand to her house just in case the witch was able to read the magic signature of the device. She used the bathroom in her office to clean up and brush her hair and then called Cerbie to her from his room here at the office, grateful that their psychic connection allowed her to do so.

"I need you to be a distraction, Cerbie. I don't want her to know anything about the wand."

He cocked his head ears up. "You found it?"

"Yeah."

"You aren't going to give it to her?"

"No."

His ears wiggled in surprise.

"It's too dangerous, Cerbie."

"Duh. It's probably not the only dangerous thing they have in their arsenal. It just surfaced while you're involved with someone it could hurt."

"Not just hurt, Cerbie. End. It could wipe vampire kind out. As drunk as Seymour was, he understood what was happening. The others are trying to take over while the High Priestess is gone. We have to hold the fort until she gets back."

"So you trust her to oversee things once she's back?"

"I haven't made up my mind, but I know I don't trust the witches who are at the helm right now with something that could possibly sway the balance between one species and another. If we allow that to happen, we'll be no better than the humans who are killing off one species after another without conscience."

"Okay. Let's do this thing."

She picked up the file and left her office to march down the hall to the conference room. She held the door open for Cerbie to follow her into the room. Once again the smell of magic followed the woman. What was she up to? "Hello, Ms. Ghostly."

Glendora rose from her seat, her posture perfect for showing off her figure. "Tell me there is good news."

Zaira pulled out a chair from the table but didn't sit down. She arranged her features "I do have some news for you. I was able to track down Seymour Hurst. He is diligently drumming up attendance for the WaVeS ball, just as he should be. I'm convinced he has nothing to do with the disappearance of the wand. I'm also monitoring several burglaries of other magical artifacts that have taken place in the area." Which was true. "They may be connected to the disappearance of the wand."

"I don't need maybes, Ms. O'Shea. I need the wand."

"It's more difficult than you realize to trace something when it isn't being used. It leaves no signature until it is. No one has put the article on any of the black market sites to sell, which would have been helpful, because then I'd be able to trace the transaction. Whoever has it is keeping it to themselves."

Cerbie went around the table and barked at the witch, his stub of a tail wiggling like mad.

"What does he want?"

"He is greeting you and wants a pat on the head."

He sat down and grinned, showing off his teeth. Glendora shot him a wary look. "He looks like he might bite me."

"Cerbie has a soft spot for the ladies. He would never bite you."

He rolled over and presented his belly to be rubbed.

"He's showing subservience to you."

Glendora smiled, obviously liking that. She bent and rubbed his chest and belly. He bounced to his feet and rubbed against her ankles like a cat. She patted his head.

"Is there any news about Councilwoman Nelson's return?" Zaira asked.

"No, thank the Goddess. That is not what we want at this time."

Yeah. Big surprise. "I promise my team and I are doing everything we can. I tasked Roger, one of our most gifted investigators, to monitor the black market sale of magical devices." She slid the sheet across to Glendora. "These are the only things sold in the two weeks since we first accepted the case. You may want to check the list for other things that might have been stolen from the Council's storage facility. Even though you weren't aware of the wand's loss, there may be something else you recognize from the list."

Glendora reached for the paper, but before her hand made contact, she jerked her attention downward. "Oh, my Goddess, what's he doing now?"

Zaira followed the woman's attention. Cerbie had wrapped his front paws around the woman's leg and was humping it for all he was worth. His lips were pulled back from his teeth and his tongue hung out.

"Get him off me!" Glendora shook her leg, but the dog held on, his little hips going like a piston. The witch jumped around on one foot and swung her leg in an attempt to unseat him. He panted, making noises like he was about to....

Zaira stared at him in shock. She'd told him to be a distraction, but he was taking that to whole new heights. "Cerbie, stop that. Bad dog!"

Cerbie ran his long tongue up the woman's leg.

Glendora squealed. "Ewww, I have dog cum on my leg." She poofed.

Cerbie fell over on his side. His grin was evil as he picked himself up, gave a shake, and pranced about in a circle, his stub of a tail pointed straight up. "I'm the man."

The sound of a crash came from the reception area, and the walls of the conference room shook. Voices carried down the hall. Calamity's panicked cry triggered all of Zaira's protective instincts, and she popped into reception with Cerbie. His small body vibrated with a businesslike growl as they both took in the six warlocks from the Council dressed in their robes, facing off with five vampires dressed in Versace suits and snowy white silk shirts.

Power singed the air from both sides. Fangs and wands had been drawn. There was a great deal of hissing going on, though no blood had been shed. Not yet.

The door hung askew on its hinges. Darkness had descended while she'd been in the conference room with Glendora, and she hadn't even noticed.

Calamity cringed back in the corner, out of the line of

fire. Zaira checked her for any injuries and, with a wave, transported the young witch to her side. "Go home Calamity."

"But, I can't leave you here alone. Roger's already left, and Calista is out on an investigation."

"What about Aileen?"

"She's still here."

"Pop into her office and tell her we're in need of some of her most potent pixie dust. No way will we allow them to destroy my office."

Calamity grinned and disappeared.

She waved a hand and fixed the damaged door. A tall, dour-looking vampire stepped forward. "We are here for the wand. We know you have it."

Chris would never turn her into the Vampire Council. His disdain for them would prevent it. If he'd already discovered she'd taken it, he'd come after it himself. "It isn't here. My team and I are still looking for it."

"You cannot give the wand to them." Archie, the warlock who'd signed the contract with their agency stepped forward. "You've been paid to find it for the Witch Council. Your loyalty should be to us."

Adcock interrupted him. She recognized him from Chris's description. "You have been seen with Christophe."

She felt the breeze from tiny wings and a high-pitched, cheerful voice buzzed in her ear. "Incoming."

A glimmer like a soap bubble settled just above the

vampire's head then flitted away. Zaira eased up her shields to protect Cerbie and herself from the dust.

"Yes. Chris hired me to help him rescue his uncle. He was being held against his will. You wouldn't know anything about that would you, Mr. Adcock?"

The vampire narrowed his eyes and flashed his fangs. "You will soon learn not to interfere in vampire business, Ms. O'Shea."

"You will soon learn not to come in here and try and destroy mine."

She could tell the moment the Pixie dust hit him. He gave a wiggle she doubted was a dance move, followed by a thrust as he clamped the cheeks of his ass together. He thrust his hand down the back of his pants and started scratching his ass.

Archie, the warlock Glendora had ordered to sign the contract, used the edge of a door facing to scratch between his shoulder blades, and suddenly sprung around to scratch his front in a move that any pole dancer would have envied.

Like flea-infested dogs, vampires and witches alike started wiggling and scratching with manic glee. The male witches bailed out of their robes like strippers at a burlesque. The vampires followed suit, shedding their elegant clothes and rolling around on the ground and digging at their skin. She almost felt sorry for them. Almost. She had never seen so much white skin or so many skinny asses in her life. Though the vampires did seem to have a little more muscle.

Cerbie rolled on his back, making noises somewhere between a bark and a growl, slobber flying in all directions. For a moment Zaira thought he was having a seizure, until she heard his mirthful snorts.

Eileen hovered in front of her shield. Her tiny, totally feminine figure was dressed in pink lace, her blond hair hanging in ringlets around her shoulders. Her wings flapped so fast they were just a blur. "This is going to last a while, and when they finally stop scratching they'll be too exhausted to do much damage. I'll stick around until they stagger out of here."

"I owe you, Eileen."

"You've saved my pixie ass more than once. That's why we're a team."

It wasn't until she was driving home that Zaira thought to wonder where Chris had been during all of the excitement. He had been entirely too quiet since she left him earlier. The chances that he hadn't discovered the wand was missing yet were slim and slimmer.

If he wasn't at her office, then it meant he might be at her house. She'd hidden the wand well, and he didn't have the box to track it. He wouldn't know where to look. But magic was unpredictable.

Zaira slammed her foot down on the gas pedal and screeched into her neighborhood on two wheels.

Chapter 12

C HRIS STIFLED HIS laughter while he watched the Council members dig at themselves like monkeys.

He'd been a little concerned as he watched the Vampire and Witch Council members fight over who was going to enter the office first. He hovered, concerned for Zaira's safety, and waited to intercede if he was needed. He should never have doubted Zaira. She was one of the strongest witches he'd ever met. Watching her deal with both Councils in short order thrilled him.

But both Councils were going to be more than furious with her once they recovered. He had to get the wand back. As long as she had it, she'd be in danger. She was going to be in danger even if she didn't have it. Witches and vampires had long memories, and their grudges and feuds made the Hatfield and McCoy conflict look like a minor disagreement.

And she would never keep the wand at her office, where all sorts of preternatural creatures wandered through. No, her house was the likeliest place.

He turned west and put on some speed as he ran and leapt along the tops of the buildings. He stepped off the side of the last tall building and landed in an alley about a block from her house. Jogging across the street, he checked for anyone watching, then once again broke into a fast clip, following the sidewalks of the subdivision.

He had no trouble picking the lock to her back door, and no wards kept him from entering the premises. Perhaps because he'd already been invited in. He heard the hum the moment he stepped inside the kitchen. The sound actually resonated inside his head, like a bee trapped in his ear. When it was cushioned inside the wall between layers of insulation, the wand's tone had been dulled. Here it was pervasive, which made it more difficult to track. He opened the oven. The microwave, the refrigerator, but the sound never changed.

He searched every cabinet and every drawer of the pocket-sized kitchen. It had to be right here in front of him. Perhaps it was hidden under a cloaking spell.

It reacted to vampires. So it would react to him. He thrust his hand out, palm down and passed it over some of the same areas he had already hunted. When he placed his hand inside the oven, the sound grew louder, as did the creepy sensation along his palm.

He hadn't tried to bake the damn thing. Maybe he could just turn the oven on and see if the heat could accomplish what all his tools couldn't. The problem with that was if it backfired, as it had in his garage, it might take out Zaira's kitchen.

He reached into the oven again and, even though it looked empty, his fingers brushed against an object. He gripped it and withdrew it from the oven. As soon as it passed the open door the box appeared, solid, real, with symbols carved into it matching the wand. He opened the box and the wand lay inside. He extracted it, and immediately the symbols on the exterior of the box started moving. He placed it back inside and they stilled.

Was that how Zaira had found the wand at his house? Had he taken the box, she would never have been able to track the wand. He wouldn't make that mistake again.

There had to be somewhere he could hide the wand where no one would ever find it again. A bottomless sinkhole. The depths of an active volcano filled with lava. Somewhere where its destructive force could never be used against anyone.

"I won't ask how you got into my house," Zaira's voice came from the kitchen doorway.

Damn. She'd sneaked up on him again. He turned to face her and found her holding a wand.

Some of the hurt and disappointment he'd felt earlier rushed back. "I can't believe you slept with me so you could steal the wand."

Her features blanked for a moment. "The wand had nothing to do with my sleeping with you. Not directly."

"What do you mean?"

"It isn't important anymore. We both know this, whatever this is, could never go beyond what it did. There's too much pressure from both witch and vampire communities for it to be anything else."

"Coward," he accused. "You're just like all the others. If a guy doesn't have a beating heart, he isn't capable of feelings. Is that what you think?

Her delicate jaw hardened. "No. And I'm not a coward. I'm the first witch to hire a diverse group to work under one roof. I have no bias or prejudice against anyone. If I did, I'd never have let you touch me."

Was that a small catch he heard in her voice?

She straightened her posture and pushed her shoulders back.

"I can't let you take the wand, Chris. It's much too dangerous."

He stepped back toward the kitchen door and heard the locks flick back in place. Locks wouldn't keep him in, but she could put up a barrier. "I can't let you have it for the same reason. If the Witch Council gets their hands on it, vampire kind will no longer exist, and there will be no one left strong enough to hold them in check. Humankind will have no chance against them."

She countered with, "If the Vampire Council gains access to it, they'll use the power to do away with all witches, no matter how many of their own kind they have to sacrifice. Vampires can make vamps more quickly than witches can be naturally born. And it takes so damn long for us to come into our power."

Her power whipped through the room like a stiff breeze. "Don't make me hurt you, Chris. I don't want to hurt you."

"I would never hurt you. But I'm not giving the wand to you, Zaira."

A thin sliver of power came at him and he raised the box to protect himself. The stream ricocheted off the box, then off the door facing in a flash of light.

Zaira yelped, staggered back, and braced a hand on the small dining room table just outside the door. She dropped the wand and it rolled to the floor.

Concerned, Chris rushed to her side. "Where are you hurt?"

"None of your business." But she was rubbing her behind.

He set the box on the table. "Here, let me see." He started to raise her skirt.

She slapped at his hand.

A small white blur lunged at him and grabbed his pants leg. The tug and jerk weren't strong enough to unbalance him, but were an aggravation when he was attempting to focus on Zaira. He reached down and grabbed the dog by his stub of a tail like it was a handle, brought him to face height and snarled, "Stop it, you little shit. She's hurt."

He set the dog on the table like a teacup. Cerbie plopped his butt down and remained silent.

"The wand has a self-defense mechanism in place that

reflects back any aggression toward it. I almost staked myself through the head with a hammer trying to destroy it."

Zaira's hazel gaze bored into his. "You mean it can't be destroyed."

"Correct. I'm almost positive at this point that it can't be. I thought about turning on the oven and letting it bake, but I was afraid it might blow up your kitchen." He placed a hand on her posterior and rubbed the rounded curve of her buttocks. "How's it feeling?"

Her cheeks flushed and she sidestepped away from him. "The pain is going away.

"I can kiss it and make it better." He bit his lip to keep from smiling.

At her continued embarrassed silence, he smiled. "I saw the Councils arrive at your office, and stuck around in case you needed assistance. You handled them rather well."

"Not without a little help from my friends." She rubbed Cerbie behind the ears, then lifted him and placed him back on the floor.

"We can't allow either Council to get their hands on the wand, Zaira. It's too powerful, and too deadly. You know they'll use it against each other as a weapon."

"I know. But if it can't be destroyed... What can we do with it?"

He drew a relieved breath. At least she was open to working with him instead of against him. "I thought about dropping it down a volcano, but it would probably blow a hole through the earth. I thought about dropping it into the middle of the ocean, but what if it washed ashore again, or has a negative effect on the sea life? It puts out a low-pitched hum that might draw them to it."

"Cerbie do you hear it?" Zaira asked.

He growled.

"He says yes, he hears it." She shook her head. "So we can't do away with it anywhere it'll be around animals, either. Someone's familiar could lead them right to it."

"While both the Councils are recovering from whatever you did to them, I have to leave with it and find a safe place to hide it." He looked into her eyes. "You know it's the best thing to do."

"You're not going alone." She laid both hands on his chest. "You might run into trouble. It's always good to have a witch on board."

He searched her face. "You didn't share yourself with me to get the wand, did you?"

"No." Her eyes grew suspiciously bright. "I shared myself with you because I thought you might never want to see me again once I betrayed you by stealing the wand. I thought if I had it, the Vampire Council couldn't stake you, because there'd be no way for them to know you stole it."

Excitement jump-started his heart, and it thudded against his ribs. He tugged her in tight against him and kissed her. "You're the first woman, witch, I've felt like this about in over a hundred years. To hell with how other witches feel about vampires, and screw how my species feels about witches. It's just us, Zaira."

She cupped his face in her hands and kissed him. "I agree."

"It may take a while to find a safe place to hide the wand. We'll have to be gone a while."

"I know."

"It could get dangerous. Both Councils will come after us. They won't forget how you got the best of them."

"I know."

Cerbie suddenly ran around in circles barking, his front legs bouncing off the ground with his adamancy.

"What's he saying?"

"He's saying he's not being left behind, and that we need to get our asses in gear. He hears a car pulling into the driveway."

Chris crossed the living room at vampire speed and looked out the window. "Shit! It's Adcock's goons. Can you teleport us to my house so we can get the car?"

Zaira held out a hand. "Let's go."

Chapter 13

"**G**O AHEAD, THROW it in," Chris encouraged. "No one but the two of us.... sorry, Cerbie...three of us will ever know it's here."

Zaira stared at the small cemetery plot. The smell of freshly turned soil and cut grass hung in the air.

"They're on our tail, Zaira. We have to hide it somewhere before they catch up with us."

She knelt and raised the indoor/outdoor carpeting covering the hole, and the supports that would hold the coffin during the service until it was lowered into the grave. She slipped the box beneath and let it go. She heard a soft thump as it hit the bottom of the six-foot deep grave.

Maybe, just maybe, they'd found a place to hide the damn thing.

"Why do you think this is going to work when letting it float over Niagara Falls didn't?" she asked.

"Because they're going to lower a casket on top of it, and it won't be able to get out from under it. Between the concrete vault, the casket, and the body, it will be weighted down and won't be able to move."

She hoped he was right. They'd been driving for two weeks trying to get rid of the wand, and somehow it always ended up right back in Chris's car. They hadn't been able to figure out how.

"The dragons could be the key-holder to keep the peace. If this doesn't work, maybe we can try them."

"It's a grave responsibility. A responsibility I'm starting to believe we're stuck with if this doesn't work."

She suddenly realized that, no matter how patient and indefatigable he seemed, he was just as weary as she and Cerbie were.

"Let's go wait in the car," he suggested.

They walked down the hill. With his hand resting on the small of her back, which was only one of the many courtesies he showed her, she felt how cherished she was. When he opened the door to the car for her, she paused to stroke his cheek. His beard felt springy and soft against her palm, and she rose on tiptoe to kiss him.

She had fallen for a vampire. With all her heart.

"I've enjoyed every moment of this adventure."

He smiled. "Even when the Hell's Angels Shifters were chasing us on their Harleys to turn us in?"

"Even then."

"Even when we hit that squall out in the ocean and you were seasick?"

"Weeelllll, not so much that particular part of it. It would have been worth it if the wand had stayed buried on that deserted island."

"Yeah, it would have."

She tilted the seat forward so Cerbie could jump in back.

Cerbie climbed into the back window. "Here come the hearse and mourners. Why don't we just drive away and see what happens?" he asked.

"Because unless everything has been placed in the grave to hold the box down, it will be back in the car in a shake and shiver," Zaira replied.

"Maybe with a fresh soul hanging over it, it won't notice we're gone," he said.

Chris got into the car.

Zaira twisted around to look at Cerbie. "What do you mean a *fresh soul*?"

"The fellow who's passed away is still hanging around. He's following his family up the hill to the gravesite."

"Oh, no. No-no-no-no."

"What's happening?" Chris asked.

"Cerbie says there's a fresh soul hanging around the burial site. What did the document about the wand say about human souls?"

His brows rose. "It didn't say anything about them."

"What if it just goes into soul-swallowing mode?"

Chris looked up the hill at the pallbearers carrying the coffin, a thoughtful frown tightening his mouth and brow.

"It's not like the guy's going to climb into the grave and back into his body," Cerbie said, sounding bored. "As long as he stays away from the wand, he'll be okay."

Chris brushed her arm with a hand. "Someone has to direct the wand before it turns on, Zaira. I'm certain of it."

She drew a relieved breath. "That's good."

The pallbearers made it to the top of the hill and set the casket on the supports. The mourners took their place in fold-out chairs beneath the small, open-sided tent. The minister took position before the casket and began the service.

"Let's go," Cerbie urged.

Chris reached for the key and started the car. He pulled around the narrow cemetery road and out the entrance. They remained silent as the miles passed.

Zaira gave a sigh as the tension drained from her. This might actually work. Chris smiled and reached for her hand.

She looked over her shoulder to find Cerbie stretched out in the back window, soaking up the sun.

Five minutes later when he barked she thought he was dreaming. "It's coming. It looks like a flying turd coming right at us."

Chris looked in the rearview mirror and his eyes widened. "Shit!"

"See, I told you," Cerbie answered.

He stomped on the gas, and the Aston Martin took off like a rocket. Zaira tightened her seat belt and braced a hand on the dashboard while Chris took a deep curve at a hundred miles an hour. The box seemed to catch the flow of air over the vehicle and cruise along ten feet behind them. After five minutes of racing ahead of it and gaining no ground, Zaira placed a hand on Chris's arm.

"Stop. You're not going to lose it."

He swore and pulled over into the emergency lane. He got out of the car and stood facing the hovering, box with the door open.

Zaira heard a high-pitched whine above the whoosh of passing traffic.

"Yeah, yeah. Stop bitchin' and get in the car." He motioned to the back seat. It flew through the open space and landed in Zaira's lap." She automatically put a hand atop the lid. It vibrated beneath her touch.

What if there was more to the wand than just being a weapon? It had a personality like a person. It had attached itself to them. But they weren't strong enough to keep it safe. They had to find someone strong enough who was, who didn't have a dragon in this fight. In fact, the dragons would be perfect.

THE KING OF the Dragons didn't live in a cave. He lived in a mansion. The car idled noisily while they took in the sprawling structure, which was easily as big as one of Scryville's city blocks.

"All they can do is tell us to go away," Chris said.

"Or they could fry us on the spot."

"I don't think they're known for frying people indiscriminately. Besides, they have no reason to. We're not a danger to them."

Zaira sat back in her seat. "Well, we can't just sit in the car admiring their house. We might as well go ahead and see if he'll speak to us."

Chris drove forward and stopped at the gate, where a huge W in the center of the wrought iron barrier mirrored the distant Colorado mountain peaks.

Her hands trembled and she cupped them in her lap. They'd come so far. Where would they go from here if Brandon Winslow wouldn't help them?

Chris pushed the button on the pole-mounted speaker close to the gate.

"May I help you?" a female voice answered.

"My name is Chris Bakas. I have Zaira O'Shea with me. We're from Scryville, Kentucky, and we'd very much like to speak to Brandon Winslow."

"One moment please."

Zaira reached for Chris's hand.

"When the gate opens, please pull up the drive to the front door."

They both breathed a sigh.

Cerbie snorted from the back seat. "That was too easy. They were expecting us."

Zaira translated what he said to Chris.

"He may be right. But it will be worth it just to sit in a

chair for a while instead of this bucket seat."

She couldn't argue with that.

Chris parked in front of the huge double doors.

She felt stiff as a poker as she swung her legs out the open car door and got out. Cerbie headed for the landscaping as soon as she let him out of the car. She ignored him while she picked up the wand, which was nestled in its box on the floor of the car, and tucked it under her arm.

The door swung open before they ever reached it. A very tall, very curvaceous woman stood just inside waiting for them. Her dark hair, cut very short, curled against her head in attractive swirls, and her skin glowed snow white against a stark black gown. As beautiful as she was, her most startling feature was her tawny-gold eyes.

"Welcome to Cliff House. I'm Helena," she said as they entered the foyer with Cerbie close behind.

"Nice to meet you," Chris extended his hand. Zaira followed suit.

An impressive vaulted ceiling soared thirty feet overhead, where an octagon-shaped skylight twenty feet in diameter glowed with the last of the evening light.

Zaira was surprised when Helena bent and gave Cerbie a rub and pat, then straightened. "If you'll follow me, I'll take you to Brandon."

They followed Helena down a long corridor, past white walls, hardwood floors, and gray wainscoting, until she stopped before a door and gave it a tap. When a male voice invited them in, she opened the door and stood back to allow their party of three to enter. "Would you like to come with me, Cerbie? I'll make you a snack."

Zaira hoped Helena meant to feed him and not snack on him herself.

His doggy grin stretched across his muzzle, showing every one of his tiny, sharp teeth.

"I'll take that as a yes. Come along."

He waddled off with her, his tongue hanging out the side of his mouth.

He didn't normally trust anyone so immediately, so he was either besotted, or he could read Helena better than she could.

With one last backward glance, she followed Chris into an enormous office lined with bookcases.

A man rose from behind his desk and approached them. Zaira tilted her head back to look into Brandon Winslow's yellow-brown eyes. Did all dragon shifters have eyes like him and Helena? The shifter's height and size gave him an intimidating presence even when he wasn't in his scaly, fire-breathing, winged form. His dark hair lay thick against his head and, with careless gesture, he brushed it back off his forehead with a hand the size of a catcher's mitt.

He introduced himself, then offered his hand, first to Zaira then to Chris. "We've been expecting you."

Cerbie was right.

"Come, have a seat. You've been traveling for days and

have to be tired."

He had no idea.

Instead of the chairs in front of his desk, he directed them to the sofa facing a large fireplace, and took a chair to the right.

"Is that the wand?" he asked, nodding toward the box resting in her lap.

"Yes."

"May I see it?"

What was to keep him from turning the wand on them? But then what would be the point? He was powerful enough to reduce them both to ashes in seconds. She rose to place the carved box in his hands and watched while he opened the lid and removed the wand. It looked like a twig in his hand.

"Such a small thing to cause such a ruckus."

"Yes, it is."

"I can feel its power." He placed it back in its box and returned it to her. "I know why you've come, and I'm sorry to say I can't help you."

Disappointment, bitter and painful, gripped Zaira's throat, making it impossible to speak.

"Why not?" Chris asked. "You would be neutral ground, Mr. Winslow. And no one would dare attempt to take it from your possession."

"There's only one problem, Chris. May I call you Chris?"

"Sure."

"I've signed a treaty with both the witches and the vampires that prevents me from interfering in any witch or vampire business or disagreements."

He had to help them. He had a moral responsibility to do so. "Please. We're not just talking about a disagreement. We're talking about the possible genocide of an entire species, Mr. Winslow."

"That's only if it falls into the wrong hands. And at the moment it's obviously in the right ones."

Chris leaned forward in his seat. "We can't fight off the two councils, Mr. Winslow. Not alone."

"That's why I'm going to give you an address where you can meet Head Councilwoman Nelson."

Beating back tears of relief, Zaira rushed to hug Chris. "Thank the Goddess!"

THE WINSLOWS WERE cordial and entertaining, and the dinner fantastic. The bag of O-positive dragon blood they presented to Chris was rich, tasty, and pumped energy into his flagging system.

But Zaira started fading fast right after dinner, and Cerbie, who was lying on his feet, snored so loudly Chris had to cover his smile with a napkin. "If you wouldn't mind, Brandon, Helena, I think we need to retire. If we're going to leave for Massachusetts tomorrow, we'll need our rest."

"We understand." Helena rose. "We'll say goodnight,

then. But we're early risers, so we'll share breakfast with you before you leave. The children can join us then."

Zaira pushed her chair back. "We'll look forward to meeting them. We really appreciate your hospitality."

Chris bent to scoop Cerbie up. The dog mumbled sleepily. "I'll take him out while you go on to our room. We'll be there in a moment."

The Colorado evening would have been chilly had he not been impervious to the cold. Chris took a seat on the steps while the dog did his business. He came back to sit next to him. "I love her, Cerbie. No matter what we face along the way, I'll protect her."

Cerbie leaned against him.

Chris put his arm around him. "We'll protect her."

The two wandered back to the room together, where Cerbie dragged his pillow into the walk in closet and was once again snoring by the time Zaira emerged from the bathroom, rosy from a shower and bringing with her the smell of cinnamon.

Chris popped in to take a shower and brush his teeth, and she was sleeping soundly when he came out to join her. He reminded himself that Zaira had the frailty of being closer to human, and needed to rest. He could slake his hunger for her when they'd completed their mission.

He slid beneath the covers and concentrated on slowing his breathing. His body no longer followed the rules of a traditional vampire sleep cycle. He rose early to teach his classes, and often worked until six, fed, then listened to music. Three hours' rest was all he ever needed, but with the dragon blood singing through his veins, it took some time to turn his mind off and will away his need for her.

He woke when Zaira rose and disappeared into the bathroom, then returned. She slipped back into bed and curled up against him to snuggle. Privacy had been in short supply while traveling with Cerbie and the wand, and a stolen kiss and a quick grope were all they'd managed since making love at his house.

"I shut the door to the closet, and the wand is in the top drawer of the dresser," she whispered in his ear.

The heat of her breath against his skin was all it took to send the blood in his system rushing south. He brushed his mouth over hers and reached for her. She wiggled in close, molding her body tightly against his. When she pulled the drawstring to his pajama bottoms and freed him, his heart began to beat.

He took her lips with a hunger he couldn't control, and his tongue sought hers at the same moment her hand closed around him. He groaned at the pleasure of her touch as she stroked and caressed him.

He peeled her sleep shirt up over her head and off. Pressed his mouth to her throat, her shoulder, and eased her back to cup her breast and take the nipple into his mouth, tonguing it. Her back bowed as she raked her fingers through his hair.

"I can't touch you enough. I've never wanted a woman as much as I want you," he whispered. He kneaded her breast while his lips came back to hers.

"I feel the same, Chris. Come inside me."

He freed himself from his pajama pants and settled between her legs. He kissed her again, tenderly, as he guided his erection inside her as slowly as he could. The sensation of her body gripping his nearly sent him over the edge, but he beat it back with vampire control.

"Let me hold you like this for a moment," she murmured. She ran her hands up and down his back as her lips and tongue answered the seductive tenderness of his. He waited for her to move beneath him before starting their inevitable dance of passion.

He stretched it out as long as he could, keeping his movements slow and measured, building their pleasure, until the even sound of her breathing changed to ragged pants. His control wavered, and he thrust deeper. When she cried out, he lost control, and his own pleasure rolled over him, stealing the steady beat of his heart.

Afterwards he was reluctant to move and break the deep intimacy they had discovered together.

"We're going to find Councilwoman Nelson, hand over the wand, and move on with our lives."

"Yes, we are."

An abrupt knock at the door startled them both. Reluctantly, Chris pulled away and rushed with vampire speed to dress.

Helena stood at the door in her robe. "Both Councils are on their way. You need to leave now if you hope to stay ahead of them. We'll stall them as long as we can."

Chris bit back an oath and turned to find Zaira already dressed. "I've teleported the bags into the trunk," she said. "I'll get the wand, you get Cerbie."

By the time they made it to the car, Helena stood next to it with a cooler. "You'll need this," she said as she passed it off to Chris. "And Brandon and one of his men are going to give you a lift down the mountain and some distance away. When all this is settled, please come back. You're welcome any time." Zaira hugged the woman and thanked her.

Chris stared at the two huge dragons waiting nearby for them to get into the car. Their wingspans were easily twenty feet across, their scales a hand's-width each, shimmering in the moonlight like they were dipped in mother-of-pearl. How could something that size be condensed into the man who greeted them the evening before?

"It's magic," Zaira said as she reached for his hand. "We need to go."

Chapter 14

ZAIRA SHIFTED IN the bucket seat and stretched. They'd been traveling the interstates for hours when they pulled off onto a rural road. Between Cerbie's hypnotic snoring rhythm in the back seat and the constant jiggle of the Aston Martin's headlights as they jounced over the many potholes in the current road they traveled, she could barely keep her eyes open.

Chris looked disgustingly fresh and alert. She felt like a leftover slice of pizza left lying in the box for about a week.

"We're almost there," he said breaking the silence.

She voiced the fears plaguing them both. "If the Councilwoman isn't there, I don't know what else to do. We can't keep running. There's no place else for us to go."

Chris lifted one hand off the wheel to reach for hers. "If news of the bounty has reached them, we might have to surrender. I heard this community is made up of nothing but preternatural beings, no humans."

"I heard that too." She looked out the window as the first houses became visible.

His fingers tightened on hers. "No matter what happens,

I want you to know, these past two weeks have meant a great deal to me. They say when you travel with someone, you really get to know them."

They had gotten to know each other. Not just from sharing their bodies, their power and her sensing things through her empathic connection. They'd talked about their pasts, their futures, and everything in between.

"I think I'm going to barf," Cerbie said from the back seat.

"Shut up, Cerbie," Zaira snapped.

"No. I mean it. I think I'm going to barf."

"You'd better pull over Chris."

He eased the car over and Cerbie had no more than jumped out than he began to gag and wretch.

Once he'd calmed somewhat, Zaira picked him up and cradled him in her lap his head over her shoulder while she soothed him.

"We're all exhausted. What we need is a good night's sleep," Chris said. "Even me. I'm getting tired of having to sleep in the trunk. Let's see if there's someplace for us to stay."

Zaira massaged Cerbie's ears. It was a bit like cuddling an overstuffed roll pillow with legs. Not that she'd ever tell him that.

He snuffled her neck.

"Feeling better?"

"Hum. The wand's purring."

"Purring?"

"Yeah."

This was getting stranger and stranger.

✧　✧　✧

CHRIS HAD NEVER seen a town quite like Salem Massachusetts. Before dusk the streets were crowded with people all dressed in costume, mostly witches. He'd read about the witch trials but it had always been an abstract thing since he hadn't been alive. It would be a great deal more personal to Zaira. He reached for her hand and gave it a squeeze.

"Are you sure about this?" he asked.

"Since Weston gave us the lead my staff has been trying to find Councilwoman, Nelson. Roger swears by this information. She's here in town, and the bartender at this pub can get in touch with her."

"Why would a witch want to come to a place where they burned witches at the stake, to take a vacation?"

"Maybe she still has family in the area."

Chris turned down a side street, he heard music playing, and followed the sound. Couples were going inside a small pub. He studied the place "You really want to take the dragon by the tail don't you?"

"Bartenders and hairdressers know everything. And though I saw a barbershop, it wasn't open."

She had a point there. He pulled the Aston Martin into the lot and parked.

"Do you feel like going in, Cerbie?" Zaira asked.

The dog growled. Chris raised his brows in question.

"He says he's good. Maybe we can get something to eat once we're through here. He's hungry."

"Sounds like a plan."

Chris handed her the wand for safekeeping while he lifted Cerbie out of the car and set him on his feet. He smoothed the dog's fur with a comforting stroke and received Cerbie's customary show of teeth that could mean friendship, or touch me again asshole and I'll chew your arm off. He could never tell.

Zaira looped her hand around his arm as they followed the little dog to the bar. "He's a little embarrassed about getting carsick and losing his cookies."

"It happens to the best of us. He's learned to tolerate me on this trip. Maybe once this is over we can go out to dinner or a movie, just the two of us, like a normal couple."

"I'd love that." Her tone held the same hope he was clinging to. They couldn't go on travelling from city to city looking for Head Councilwoman Nelson.

The interior of the bar was a great deal larger than it looked outside. The walls were paneled in warm wood. The bar, made of some dark wood gleamed with care, and the rows of bottles behind shone in a multitude of fall tones from red to gold and then some.

Chris breathed in deep so he could check the scents around him. Shifters. Every patron was a Shifter. They wouldn't like that a vampire had invaded their territory. He scanned the place for trouble.

There was a brawny guy at the second table for the doorway eyeing them. Had to be a bear Shifter.

The band was playing a country music tune, and the lead guitarist was belting the song out with all he had in a rich baritone. His thick black hair, combed back from a broad forehead, displayed a deep widows peak. Even though the guy was singing, he was watching them.

They approached the bar. "May I have a bowl of water for my dog?" Zaira asked.

The bartender, a very large man who looked like he could act as barkeep and bouncer all in one, waited on Zaira, but eyed Chris with a wary look. "Certainly, little lady." He filled and handed her the bowl.

Chris took it from her and bent to offer it to Cerbie. The dog drank deeply. He left it and stood close so no one would step on their stubby hellhound and get their ankles bitten or peed on.

"Can I get you anything else?"

"We're searching for someone who may be in the area on vacation. We were hoping she might have been in."

"Who might that be?"

Zaira leaned forward to lower her voice. "We're looking for Head Councilwoman Nelson."

Every voice stopped. The music echoed on the last note played then died away.

"Who's askin'?" The shifter who played lead guitar, set aside his instrument, leapt down from the stage, and wandered over.

Zaira glanced at Chris. He nodded. "I'm Zaira O'Shea, and this is Chris Bakas. We've recovered something that was taken from the Witch Council's storage facility, and we want to return it to the Councilwoman."

"There's a bounty on your heads. You know that, don't you?" the shifter asked.

"Yes, we know. There's been something strange going on with the Council in her absence. It might be a hostile takeover. We want put the wand in her hands and no one else's."

"Shit! She's going to be so pissed."

Chris couldn't allow Zaira to take full responsibility. He was the one who'd taken the wand. "The Vampire Council may have found out about it and are trying to take advantage. They're not far behind. If you know where she is, you need to get word to her right away."

The shifter-guitarist called two young men over and murmured something into their ears. They took out the backdoor like the hounds of hell were after them.

The sound of metal bending and glass breaking came from the parking lot, and a crowd headed for the door and looked out the windows.

Chris grasped Zaira's arm and pulled her close, the wand between them. "This is probably it, Zaira. I'll try to protect you in every way I can, but if something should happen to me, teleport out of here. Keep you and Cerbie safe. And whatever else happens, keep the wand out of their hands."

"We'll stand together. They can't harm us if we stand together."

If only that were true. Chris kissed her to reassure her, but a feeling of dread settled in his stomach. They stayed close together while they followed the shifter crowd outside.

Chris's Aston Martin had been crushed against the side of a pickup by a large black limousine. Zaira actually groaned when she saw it. "As much as I've wanted out of that car for the last week, it hurts to see it trashed."

He felt a little sick himself over what they'd done to his ride.

Seven vampires climbed out of the limo—Adcock, his minions on the Council, and his two large goons.

The seven vampires ignored the large group of Shifters as if they weren't there. "We want the wand, Christophe. Hand it over."

"I can't do that, Adcock."

A wave of snickering erupted around them.

"Did you have to add one to make sure you had one?" a voice jeered from the back of the group.

"Oh, shit!" Chris muttered. "He hates that."

Adcock looked around, his eyes glowing red. "Once I have the wand in hand, I will deal with whoever said that."

"Bring it on, Barnabas," another said closer to the front.

"Boris. He looks more like a Boris. As in bore us to death."

"Naw, I'd say Bunnicula, if it wouldn't give rabbits a bad name."

Several snickers followed that one.

"They're stalling," Zaira whispered. "Trying to give the councilwoman time to get here."

Chris nodded. "It might work for a few of minutes, but not long."

Adcock made a movement with his hand. One of his goons leaped toward them.

Zaira threw up a hand and suspended the vampire in midair. Chris sprang up and kicked him in the stomach with both feet, sending him back the way he'd come. The vampires scattered. The goon struck the hood of the limo like a bolder, making a large dent and cracking the windshield. Chris did a graceful flip and landed on his feet a short distance away.

"Make them seize,

Make them sneeze,

Make them unable to bend their knees,

And while they wheeze,

Make them freeze.

So mote it beeze."

Zaira chanted as she threw out a wave of blue-green

power.

The seven vampires started seizing and sneezing, but their feet seemed to be stuck to the asphalt.

"How long will that last?" Chris asked.

A burst of power hit Zaira, throwing her back and slamming her to the ground. Chris sped to her and felt the heat of a fireball whip past him. It exploded as it hit the parking lot, setting two cars on fire. Shifters scattered. Some ran to move their vehicles so they wouldn't be damaged in the conflagration.

Zaira lay unconscious, her face pale, a large knot forming on the side of her head just above her ear. Cerbie waddled-ran to her side and began shedding some kind of power as he stood over her.

Chris prayed to the Goddess she'd be okay. "Get out of here," he yelled at the remaining Shifters. "This isn't your fight." Some left, while others stood their ground.

Glendora and her male witch minions stood once again united. They stretched out in a line next to the vampires, who had stopped sneezing and were no longer frozen, now Zaira was unconscious. It seemed the lot of them had banded together to get the wand at any cost.

A ball of power was lobbed at him by one of the warlocks. Chris scooped up the wand in its container and turned to face the threat, striking out at it like the box was a bat. The prickly ball of static ricocheted back, right in the midst of the vampires. Two of the Council members and one of the goons fell beneath it like pins before a bowling ball.

"Thank you Chris. You're narrowing the field by taking out your own people," Glendora said with a smile.

"I'll take the rest of you out as well. You're not getting your hands on this wand. You'll destroy us all."

"You can't fight all of us off at the same time. We'll get it one way or another."

"Not while there's life left in my body."

Zaira groaned behind him and he sensed her movement.

"Get him!" Glendora yelled, throwing out a hand in his direction.

The remaining goons rushed forward, as did three other vampires. Two of the witches joined in. Chris leaped on top of one of the remaining cars and rushed to the next, and the next, with the others racing after him. He landed on a truck.

The huge, muscle-bound goon vampire was faster than he looked. He was suddenly there in front of Chris, dragging him off the vehicle by the ankle. Chris landed on his shoulder and felt the bone break. His arm went numb. He gripped the box with his remaining hand as tightly as he could, but it was wrenched from him.

"This is for Marion," the goon said in a high-pitched, girlish voice. He stomped him in the stomach, then kicked him in the back just over his kidney.

The pain drove his vision to white. Had he needed to breathe, he'd never have been able manage it.

Two of the cadaverous Vampire Council members

dragged him to his feet, none too gently, and frog-marched him back to where he'd started. He bit back a groan as they threw him down on the ground beside Zaira.

She was sitting up, and the large bump seemed to have receded, but two of the Witch Council stood over her so she couldn't get to her feet. Cerbie lay next to her on his side, his limbs limp with exhaustion. He must have healed her.

Archie had somehow gained control of the box. He held it on each end while Glendora eased the top open. She removed the wand and ran her fingertips over its carvings with a great show of interest.

As she stood over the two of them, her soulless grin brought a hollow feeling to his stomach. He looked up at Adcock. "You'd better run. She's going to turn it on all of you once she's through with us."

The other vampire flicked a glance at Glendora, wariness in his gaze.

"Not so, Christophe. But the first one who'll die is that traitorous bitch, Zaira. We have to set an example so no other witch will ever defy the Council again."

Chris slipped an arm around Zaira, and she rested her head against his shoulder. Her skin looked milky white, and her hazel gaze held steady on his. "I love you, Chris."

The warlocks and vampires shifted away from Glendora, their anxious attention directed at the weapon in her hand. She came to stand over him and Zaira. She interrupted before he could say anything. "This wand hasn't been used in nearly four hundred years. You should feel honored to be the first to be sacrificed to it in such a long time."

Glendora pointed the wand at Zaira.

"For all the strife.

You will forfeit a life.

To pay the toll.

Will cost one soul.

This is for me,

So mote it be."

Chris rolled toward Zaira, covering her. "I love you, Zaira."

The power hit him between his shoulder blades, and he bowed his back in pain and cried out. Then the strength drained from his arms, his legs, every part of him, and he slumped, his head resting against her shoulder. He wished he could draw one last breath so he could experience her cinnamon scent one last time.

He was bathed in pain as his soul broke loose from his body. His vision narrowed, and he was suddenly rushing toward a tunnel that swallowed him.

Chapter 15

ZAIRA WAILED IN pain and grief as she held Chris's limp body and rocked him. Tears burned her eyes and streaked down her cheeks. Though Cerbie had healed her head, it still pounded.

She wiggled out from underneath Chris's weight and turned him so she could see his face. His beautiful gray eyes were vacant, his features wooden now the last spark of life had been drained from them.

She shook as though her body were wired to electricity, grief and rage building inside her. "You vicious, heartless, prick-teasing bitch." She swept the men standing around her with a scathing look. "She'll kill you all, and you'll stand there and let her while you stare at her boobs."

Her rage died as quickly as it had spiked. She pressed her hands against Chris's chest and poured her magic into him. He wasn't healing himself. Without his soul, perhaps he couldn't. Her shoulder ached as she knitted the broken bones there.

"He's gone. He has no soul." Glendora circled the two of them.

Her back felt like it might break while his bruised kidney healed. She felt every bump and bruise drained of their soreness because she experienced them all as they healed, but she didn't feel him inside the shell of his body.

"The wand swallowed it," the bitchy witch taunted.

Cerbie staggered to his feet and came to lean against her. "He's gone."

She thought her heart might actually break.

"What is going on here?" A female voice demanded.

Zaira looked up and blinked her eyes to clear her tear-blurred vision. A slender witch of about thirty-five stood outside the circle of vampires and warlocks. Her blond hair flowed over her shoulders in heavy waves. She looked all the world like Glinda the good witch of the South from the Wizard of Oz. Except she wore a power suit of fine silk and a blouse with a scooped neckline. Two inch Gucci heels of butter soft leather sheathed her feet.

"Is that vampire dead?" She took several bold steps through the crowd who stood around watching.

The witch's eyes widened as she saw Glendora with the wand. She stretched out a hand and the instrument flew through the air and she caught it. "What have you done?"

"I only sought to punish the vampire responsible for stealing the wand and the witch responsible for keeping it from the Council."

"Liar." Zaira staggered to her feet. "You killed Chris. And you reveled in it. You enjoyed seeing him suffer." She turned her attention to the witch. She had to be the Head Councilwoman. There was too much fear on all the male witches' faces for her to be anyone else. "He died protecting me. It was me she wanted to kill. I didn't trust her or the rest of them, and we came to give the wand to you for safekeeping." She motioned toward the male witches. "We tried to hide the wand away, but it kept coming back to us."

"Did it, now?" Councilwoman tilted her head. She studied the wand through narrowed eyes.

"Please. Can you help him?" Zaira pleaded. A sense of urgency gripped her, hard. Without his soul his body would start to… She didn't want to think about what would happen.

The witch frowned. "Perhaps."

Zaira's anger rose again at the witch's malevolence. She was the strongest witch in the world, why wouldn't she help? Zaira balled her fists in frustration and fresh tears streamed down her face. "Adcock blackmailed Chris into stealing the wand. He held his uncle hostage until he did it."

The Councilwoman's sharp blue gaze fastened on Adcock. "Harry, it appears you have been a bad boy."

"Harry Adcock," crowed one of the shifters, standing along the periphery of the parking lot. All the rest laughed and jeered.

The Vampire flashed his fangs at them, but remained where he was.

Councilwoman Nelson turned so suddenly Glendora

gasped. "I told you to keep an eye on things. Not to go through the treasury."

"We didn't."

The Councilwoman raised a brow and the wand. "I know where I left things, Glendora." She looked around, scanning the group of warlocks. "Where is Seymour?"

Silence met the inquiry.

Zaira answered her. "He's at a hotel outside of Transylvania College drumming up participation for the WaVeS celebration—among other things."

"Why is it this young witch seems to know more about my Council than the rest of you do?"

"Seymour!" She said the warlock's name and he suddenly appeared, his pants halfway up, his bony shoulders poking out of a wife-beater T-shirt.

He hastily jerked his pants in place, zipped them, and brushed a hand over his disheveled hair. "Yes, Madame. What may I do for you?" He sounded a little out of breath.

"I won't ask what you've been doing. In return, you will tell me what they have on you to force your cooperation." She pointed the wand at Glendora and the warlocks. Everyone dived for cover behind vehicles except Glendora. She raised her chin and glared at Seymour.

"Uh. Uh." Seymour stuttered.

"I suggest you worry about what I may do instead of what she will," the head witch said.

"They've been going through records and the storage

facility for weeks. They've dragged out the most lethal of the weapons stored there. And the darkest of the spell books."

"She's been experimenting. Her aura is clouded by black magic," Zaira volunteered.

"Thank you, I can see that myself," the Councilwoman said. She studied Glendora, her eyes narrowed. "Have you been exploring, Seymour? I'll know if you're lying."

"No, Madame. I wanted no part of it."

"Good. You may go, Seymour."

The warlock didn't waste a second disappearing.

"It would seem while I've been vacationing, my rats have been playing, plotting, and planning."

Glendora's arrogance finally started to crack. "That isn't so. We were just curious."

"Curiosity killed the cat." The Councilwoman wiggled her fingers and in a blink Marilyn Monroe/ Glendora Ghostly was suddenly a ginger-striped cat. The animal hissed and yowled jumping in the air and twisting about. "Since you've been catting around behind my back, digging into things you shouldn't have, and leading my Council around by their peckers, you can spend some time as a feline. As can they. At least as a lowly feline, I can be certain none of you share any of the secrets you've learned from your foraging."

The whole group of male witches wandered out from behind the cars. Two were solid black and the others gray tabbies.

They started to converge on Glendora as a pack. She

hissed and struck out at them, backing away, then turned and ran. All six male cats gave chase.

Councilwoman Nelson strode to stand next to Zaira and pointed the wand at Chris's lifeless body.

"Cough it up, Dillion. Right now. We've had this conversation over and over. Wands do not swallow souls." She tilted her head as though she were listening to a conversation. "Well, she certainly won't keep you if you don't put it back. *Now, before it's too late.*"

A warm, yellow stream of power flowed from the wand to settle over Chris's body and sank below the surface. When he didn't wake, Zaira looked up at the witch.

"It will take some time for his soul to reconnect to his body. It may be a few days, or possibly even a week, but it will happen."

Zaira's tears rushed up again, her breath hitching as she tried to hold back her sobs. "If he doesn't f-feed, he'll die."

"His body will be in a state of hibernation. He won't need blood." She laid a perfectly manicured hand on Zaira's shoulder. "He'll wake up."

"Are you s-sure?"

"No. But I've done all I can."

More tears blurred Zaira's vision and ran down her cheeks, the anguish almost more than she could bear.

The vampires piled into the limo.

The Councilwoman waved her hand and the sound of the engine cranking and not starting went on and on.

"You're not getting away so easily. I promise you."

She turned her attention back to Zaira. "I'm sorry. I should have never taken a vacation. After so many years, I thought I could have a few weeks to myself. I was wrong. And you and your vampire have paid the price. When everything is back to normal, you and I will have a chat."

Zaira wasn't sure she wanted that.

"As for the wand... I'm afraid you're stuck with it. You and your vampire will have to share custody." The box appeared next to her, and she offered Zaira the wand.

"I don't want to touch it."

"It's the intent behind the use of it." She squatted to put the wand in the box. "You're powerful enough to have killed her. Why didn't you?"

"I wished I had...until you turned her into a cat." She wiped her face with her sleeve, swallowed, and began to pull herself together. "She'll suffer more being trapped like that, powerless and hunted. Besides, once you let the monster out of the box, there's no going back."

"No, there isn't. I'll be back to check up on you. But right now I have a car full of vampires to deal with, and help is on the way." She nodded toward a large man coming toward her. Not a man, a male witch. "This is Jameson Garrett, my mate. He'll see to safety and shelter while I take care of things here."

"Henry, the bartender tells me you've had a little trouble," the large witch said when he reached Zaira. He knelt beside her and took in Chris's prone, lifeless figure with one sweep. His broad shoulders looked wide enough to carry any burden, and his sapphire blue gaze held a steady strength. "I have a place for you to stay for as long as you need," he said.

Zaira nodded, sobbing while fresh tears poured down her face. She took a deep breath, gulped, and held out her hand. "Thank you. I'm Zaira."

"I'm Jim." He shook her hand with careful pressure.

"This is Chris." She swallowed and tried to control the fresh wave of grief. "And this is Cerberus." She drew Cerbie against her side.

"The dog who guarded hell." James raised a brown brow a little darker brown than his hair.

"He's distantly related."

Interested sparked in the witch's eyes. "You don't say."

James motioned to several shifters, and they rushed forward to lift Chris from the ground and put him on a stretcher. A large van pulled up beside them, and they loaded Chris into the back. James offered her a hand getting in.

"Adira will want to visit with you. I think the two of you will have a lot in common. You're both healing witches with a little something extra."

Zaira looked up and eyed him a little warily. "How can you tell?"

"After living with Adira for so many years, let's say I

have an eye for these things." He gave Cerbie a boost into the van and jerked back as the box with the wand in it zipped past him into the vehicle to land on the seat beside her. He looked at Zaira.

"It's a long story."

"You, Adira and I will catch up later," he promised and jumped behind the wheel.

Shouts of pain penetrated the closed vehicle, and she looked out to see what was happening to the vampires. They were dancing around, yelping every time their feet touched the ground, and their arms flapped like crow's wings.

"What are they doing?" she asked.

"Looks like dancing on hot coals. Adira can be creative with her ideas of punishment and justice."

"Good," she said, well satisfied. "I hope she keeps them at it a good, long time."

James laughed and pulled out of the parking lot. "Oh she will, you can bank on it."

Chapter 16

A BUZZING IN his ears jerked Chris out of a deep sleep. It was a bit like having someone who snored loudly sleeping the same room.

He opened his eyes to see light streaming into a window, bathing Zaira in a golden glow that set her red hair to gleaming with copper highlights. She wore a knee-length sleep shirt, and her hair, which was usually in a braid down her back, hung around her shoulders and down her back in waves to her waist.

Her expression was sad and her arms were wrapped around her legs, her chin resting on her knees with contemplative air. Her skin looked like silk, milk-white and flawless, her brows a slash of color over her hazel eyes.

The room they were in was a large and open. All the windows were shuttered but the one where she sat, keeping the light to a minimum.

The sound intruded again, drawing his attention away from her. It wasn't coming from her. He glanced to his left and saw the box they'd been carting around for weeks. The wand was sleeping. Wands slept? What was up with that?

"Zaira." His voice sounded raspy, like he hadn't used it in a long time.

She whirled around, her eyes going wide. "Chris!"

Her bare feet slapped the floor as she rushed to the large bed and leapt up on it. She cupped his face, smoothed his hair, undeniable joy in her expression as she pressed soft kisses all over his face.

"Thank the Goddess, you're finally awake."

She held him close, and he nuzzled his face against her breast, enjoying the womanly feel of her. The rest of his body was waking up with a vengeance.

She leaned back to look into his face. "That is not a banana in your pocket. You have no pockets in those sleep pants."

"No. No banana."

"You've been in a coma for a week. How can you even think about slipping me the banana the moment your eyes open?"

"Well, my banana is as fully awake as the rest of me...and besides, it just happens." He pulled her in close and kissed her, then suddenly what she'd said hit him. "What do you mean I've been in a coma for a week?"

"You have been. What is the last thing you remember?"

He thought about it. "I pulled over because Cerbie got carsick. Where is he?"

"He's playing with some of the shifter children in the neighborhood."

"Playing?"

"Yes, if you can even imagine that."

He couldn't. "Let's hope he doesn't teach them any swear words or how to pee on people's best clothes. What else have I missed?"

She filled him in on everything that had happened from the time they entered Salem, Massachusetts. It took several minutes for him to process everything she told him.

"You saved me, Chris. Sacrificed yourself to save my life." Her eyes turned glassy with unshed tears, and she sniffled and cleared her throat. "Do-don't you ever do that again," she sobbed.

He smoothed back a long strand of auburn hair from her cheek. "I love you, Zaira. I could never stand by and see you hurt." Nearly dying made it easy to say the words. He kissed her.

She curled in close against him. Her hazel eyes held the shadow of everything they'd experienced, and he couldn't remember.

"I love you, too. This past week, waiting for you to wake up has been…" She shook her head, but he could feel the tension in her as she struggled to suppress her emotions.

His heart was beating fast at her declaration, and he kissed her again. "I'm back now, and I'm not going anywhere." He breathed in her cinnamon and magic fragrance. And held her until he felt her relax.

"I should call the house and tell them you're awake."

"Where are we?"

"We're in a guesthouse in James's backyard. He and

Adira are over at the big house."

"It sounds like everyone is occupied." He turned to raise himself up on an elbow and looked down at her. "I love you. You love me. We're both in one piece. I think that calls for a celebration of some sort."

She cupped his face in her hands and kissed him and his erection pressed hard and insistent against her. "You're alive for us to love each other. That calls for an even bigger one."

He held up a finger. "There's just one thing I have to do first."

"What's that?"

He slid out of bed and grabbed the box on the nightstand. He went to the open window and tossed the wand out. It hovered outside in midair. "You owe me big time. You sucked my soul out. Just because I don't remember it, doesn't mean I'm not pissed about it. Go nap somewhere else for a while." He closed the window and the shutters and rushed back the bed. "He was awake and listening to everything we said. I'll be damned if he was going to listen to us make love."

Zaira laughed. "He'll be back. I'm afraid we're stuck with him. He's sort of imprinted on us."

"Forget about the wand." Chris took her back into his arms. "Think banana, Zaira."

She laughed. "No more wands, only your banana. And I'm making a wish I know will come true."

THE END

If you liked this book and want to continue
the series here are the links:

BOOK 2 OF THE HAVE WAND, WILL TRAVEL SERIES
ONCE BITTEN, TWICE SHY

Somewhere off the beaten path in Scryville, Kentucky, there's a little-visited trail that leads to a realm of vampire politics, danger and maybe even death.

Phoebe Stewart only agreed to marry Trevor Ricci to secure peace between their warring vampire clans. When her groom poisons her during the wedding ceremony, and her life expectancy falls from forever to a week, "till death do you part" takes on a whole new meaning. When she catches up with her new husband, she intends to stake and roast the traitorous, narcissistic weenie.

Especially now she's met Hunter Knox, the bad boy alpha vampire she's been waiting for her whole death.

Agent Hunter Knox works for the National Vampire Security Council. When a poison that can actually kill their species surfaces, he's dead set on finding and destroying it. But once he meets Phoebe, and realizes she only has days to live, the need for an antidote takes priority.

And the more he gets to know her, the more he suspects she may be as important to vampire kind as she's becoming to him.

BOOK 3 OF THE HAVE WAND, WILL TRAVEL SERIES
ADVENTURES OF A WITCHY WALLFLOWER

After 50 years of teaching magic-challenged witches, Madeline's found the perfect male witch to share a different kind of magic in her life. But his curse has another idea....

For fifty years Madeline Montgomery has taught magic-challenged witches how to cast spells. And she's good at it. When she loses her job at the college, she's thrown into an identity crisis. If she can't teach what will she do?

Broke and desperate, Jake Cunningham has borrowed money from the wrong witches. With a moniker like Jake The Rake floating around, he hasn't a chance of finding his next mark. Until he's made an offer he can't refuse—meet Madeline and he'll be a hundred thousand dollars richer.

When Jake shows up on Madeline's doorstep asking for her help, it's a goddess-send. While she teaches him to spell, he brings a different kind of magic into her life. For the first time she wants to throw caution to the wind and let her heart lead the way. But Jake insists he has a curse and if she gets too close she'll end up hating him.

But she's an expert at magic and a curse can be broken. Or can it?

FOR MORE INFORMATION ABOUT TERESA REASOR

Website:www.teresareasor.com

MILITARY ROMANTIC SUSPENSE
BREAKING FREE (Book 1 of the SEAL Team Heartbreakers)
BREAKING THROUGH (Book 2 of the SEAL Team Heartbreakers)
BREAKING AWAY (Book 3 of the SEAL Team Heartbreakers)
BREAKING TIES (A SEAL Team Heartbreakers Novella)
BUILDING TIES (Book 4 of the SEAL Team Heartbreakers)
BREAKING BOUNDARIES (Book 5 of the SEAL Team Heartbreakers)
BREAKING OUT (BOOK 6 of the SEAL Team Heartbreakers)
BREAKING POINT (A SEAL Team Heartbreakers Novella)
BREAKING HEARTS (Book 7 of the SEAL Team Heartbreakers)

SEALS IN PARADISE SERIES
HOT SEALS, RUSTY NAIL

PARANORMAL ROMANCE
TIMELESS
DEEP WITHIN THE SHADOWS (Book 1 of the Superstition Series)
DEEP WITHIN THE STONE (Book 2 of the Superstition Series)
WHISPER IN MY EAR
HAVE WAND, WILL TRAVEL (Book 1)
HAVE WAND, WILL TRAVEL: ONCE BITTEN, TWICE SHY (Book 2)
HAVE WAND, WILL TRAVEL: ADVENTURES OF A WITCHY
WALLFLOWER (Book 3)